THE LITERATURE

PREFERRED BY WILD BOAR

A NOVEL
BY
ALICE ECKLES

The Literature Preferred by Wild Boar is a work of fiction. Names, characters, places, and incidents either are the product of the author's imagination or are used fictitiously.

Printed in the United States of America
by Dancing Bee Press

First Printing, 2015
ISBN 978-0692349908

Author photograph by Ruth Eckles
Cover design by Margaret Jordan
Cover artwork by Alice Eckles

Dancing Bee Press
P.O. Box 443
Middlebury, VT 05753

www.alice-eckles.com

For Dad

CHAPTER 1

As soon as Charles suggested the outing, Deb heard a sound in her ears that reminded her of a bell, a soft tone coming in like a radio wave. She sensed something there as if a fish was pulling her line, a faint calling? She stood there not answering, possessed by an inner sound expanding in concentric circles.

"Think about it," Charles said. "We could go this afternoon, maybe find something we can use."

He was about to walk away from where Deb was tinkering with a motorcycle. Trying to get to know this strange gift Joe had given her.

"OK, let's go," she said as the tone in her head faded away. She wondered what she would have said if she'd heard a less pleasant sound—like the channel-less static she sometimes heard.

"It feels a little strange to go back there, but I thought we might scout out some building supplies, or at least find a tape measure," Charles said.

"It's slacker Sunday, Charles. It'll be recreational."

Deb was enjoying the ride, sitting with her arms

around Charles, her legs cradling him from behind on their recently inherited motorcycle, strands of her copper-turning-silver hair escaping to the wind. She saw a dark shape shift at the wooded edge of the old logging road that led into what was once known as the Contemplative Eco Community. There a wild boar emerged, the same size, shape, and color as the wallows their neighbor Alfred had shown them a few days ago.

The boar's tusks shone with surprising newness, like pieces in a garbage heap of a world that begs to be put back together in some way. It was the year 2045, and the world was peopled by only three thousand six hundred souls. In Middleburg there were about six hundred inhabitants.

The wild boar approached Charles Truman and Deb Exlander at a trot. Seeing the animal's chipped white tusks as he came at them, Charles assumed they were being charged. Gripping the handlebars tighter, he sped away, fearful of the unknown. Deb clung tighter too, mostly fearful of his driving.

They had heard of wild boars swimming to Vermont.

Gliding like water ballet troupes across the Connecticut River, to the land of their hearts' content. Yet they'd never before seen a wild boar, or even heard of a sighting that was believable.

The boar charged ten feet past them and then swiftly turned around to pursue them. It seemed to Charles that a powerful alien threatened to chase them into the underworld. Such was the haunted feeling that pervaded the failed Contemplative Community and their abandoned estate. Deb, though she generally liked animals, was afraid of large mammals that she didn't know, especially dangerous ones with bristly hair and tusks.

As the boar caught up to run alongside the motorcycle, Deb made an effort to look him in the eye.

Here is an animal who sees the truth in every situation and knows how to respond.

His snout, for which his whole body seemed made, pushed forward till his wide nostrils flared at Charles. Deb wondered how they would evade the boar before he started to nip Charles's knuckles.

From the Contemplative Eco Community, their path led to an abandoned construction site for a box store, the sort of indoor convenience city that was once popular, even if completely at odds with developments like the Contemplative Eco Community. With a boar in pursuit, this was becoming a landscape of obstacles.

"Watch out for your knuckles," she whisper-shouted in his ear.

Charles didn't care about his knuckles; he narrowed his already narrow eyes and hunched in closer to speed away.

"Don't distract me," he said, annoyed that his errand wasn't going as planned.

Deb had an idea. Ideas were her specialty. She had read somewhere about how to handle such difficulties with a wild boar.

"It would be better if you slowed down so he can get a good look at you and satisfy his curiosity. Then you could make a turn, but he'll keep going in the same direction," Deb instructed.

"We don't have time to mess around with this boar," Charles said. "I have a million things to do today."

"Take a deep breath and humor me. I really believe this will work."

Charles slowed and the boar slowed too. The boar grunted his satisfaction as he inspected the motorcycle and its occupants. Charles made a right turn, and that was the last they saw of the boar until a week or so later.

There was a place in the forest where Deb liked to forage for mushrooms, goldenseal, and ginseng. Many years ago Deb and Charles had started growing useful forest plants and fungi in a manner that simulated the wild. Often Deb went there to gather birch bark for starting campfires, and to take the pulse of the seasons. It was summer, but a cold snap could pop out from summer days, breaking summer's relative ease. That was partly why she was watchful of her forest, why Charles was watchful of his bees. There wasn't anything you could do about the unpredictability of the weather, but it seemed to help to listen closely. We are all in it together, in this symphony of sympathy. So Deb checked on things in the wild that ostensibly took care of themselves, a wild world that she had encouraged and helped create. What the forest had to teach was endless. It was her paradise.

She sat on the flat face of a rock off to the side of a path. She was there doing Reiki and chanting, when a ray of sunlight came down and spread its warmth over her. She stated her intention to send protective and healing energy to her daughter, who was traveling with her daredevil husband again. Once she settled into a peaceful meditation, everything around her followed. When she felt a greater presence, Deb opened her eyes. That was when she saw the wild boar snuffling acorns less than ten feet away. How had she not heard him approach? How had she missed his paired almond hoof marks? Had the boar simply appeared out of nowhere?

Deb watched the gentle quiet of his bearing as he came toward her, seemingly weightless, like an apparition. As if to bask in her peaceful aura of meditation, he came near, sidled up beside her and flopped down to rest, his weight and reality finally apparent. He must be sick, she reasoned. Animals sensed healing energy and sought it out when they were in need. She didn't know what was wrong with the boar. She only knew it was seeking the energy she was sending out. There was no thorn in his little cloven feet that she could tell. She had had the chance to look closely as he flopped over on his side.

She put her hand on him, and he seemed to melt into a deeply relaxed state. She observed him. He seemed in perfect condition physically. She suspected the hurt was on an emotional level. Pigs were smarter than dogs and had the same ability to be wild, or become tame, or to be anywhere in between. *What could the pig be upset about?*

Change, the sort of change a wild boar brought to the neighborhood with his rooting up of prestigious plants, was not always welcome. Perhaps the boar, the pig, the hog felt unwelcome, and unappreciated. Nature loved praise. It was not only humans who wanted to be adored, who wanted to be loved.

The whole point of the motorcycle ride was to have a fun adventure. The search for building supplies was just a lure, to get Charles to do something recreational. The wild boar saved the day, showing up like that and changing their direction. Otherwise Charles might have gotten sucked into an endless and depressing job, trying to salvage what was left after the death of a community he was once a part of.

Resting her hand on his back, she silently thanked the boar for changing their direction, for showing up and coming between Charles and his utilitarian list, his quicksand of things to do. She let her thanks ripple out to the Great Spirit from which the wild boar came. She stroked his eyebrows, till he was sound asleep.

Perhaps it was because she looked him in the eye, or maybe because she read about him and took the trouble to try and understand his wild boar-ness. Whatever it was, over that summer, the boar made it clear that Deb was his special human friend.

A wild boar is a fierce animal, shouldn't I be afraid?

Yet the boar seemed to want only comfort. Often he ran up to her only to lie down at her feet. His fur was bristly and his teeth were long, but he nuzzled close to Deb, and she took the hint and bent low to his level. When she sat down, he took advantage of this and laid his head on her lap. His eyebrows were far enough from his mouth to feel comfortable for Deb, and he seemed to like having them stroked. His head was heavy and he chewed in his sleep. She liked the boar but was not without squeamishness.

It doesn't seem entirely safe to be friends with a wild boar. On the other hand, if the wild boar sees me as his friend, is it safe not to be his friend? It's as if I've been drafted to be some sort of intermediary. The wild boar has made me his safe place, his "contact" in the human world. Let's face it, he digs up gardens, and he is at least potentially dangerous with his tusks, his weight, and reputation for killing hunters and the dogs of hunters. The pig is smart, all right. Up against Alfred and his dog, he chooses to attach himself to me. More than any of their neighbors, Alfred seemed strange as if from another planet and that prickled Deb in particular. Alfred was French; he still believed that France existed and defended his own mythological version of it.

A duty is something that can't be shirked, although one might not feel happy to oblige. That is how I feel about the boar. What he seeks from me, I have an obligation to give. Peace . . . one cannot withhold peace from a seeker. I recognize in him this desire.

CHAPTER 2

Did Charles ever think about where they would have ended up if they had kept going in the same direction? Some say the pig is selfish, but the pig is Christ-like. The pig attends to his inner self. Finally.

Of course, many people did continue in the same direction. Scientists and other experts warned of what would happen if we kept overfishing, overpopulating, overconsuming, overgrowing, overspending, overdosing, and we ended up pretty much in the projected disaster zone. Some people did change their ways, like Deb and Charles, and disaster had a tendency to strike unevenly anyway. So the world didn't exactly end, though the future survival of our species felt uncertain, as it was carried by so few . . . compared to our former strength in numbers.

The end feels close, like living in a meteor shower.

Deb and Charles had been among the last ones to return to the cradle of their old scrambled neighborhood after a dramatic increase in weather chaos, sunspots, and solar flares culminated in the Great Wobble. Scientists had predicted that changes in the magnetic field of the Earth would cause a sudden pole shift. But that didn't happen. Something a little different happened that could not be explained. The whole region shifted with the undulating energy of Earth, skewing the known geography into a changed version of itself. Canada's borders melted closer, taking over much of Vermont. At first it was thought to be an earthquake, but it was too orderly to be an earthquake. It was more like an intelligent being inside Earth was moving chunks like puzzle pieces: a sort of sleeping giant at work, dreaming a new world. The air above and the whole cosmos seemed to help the giant's reimagining as if invisibly unified. Humans felt a deep unspeakable smallness, perhaps irrelevance. They were like fleas on a dog, but worse, they could not even hold onto the dog.

It is embarrassing to think about what I was doing when the Great Wobble came. I was looking for a certain kind of candy. It was a hard candy with a soft chocolate center. It came in a little gold wrapper. I wanted it to feed to my imaginary fish. Of course, I would eat the candy, but the imaginary fish was part of my invented religion. God knows why I had become obsessed with getting this particular type of candy as fish food. Pips, they were called. My fish-wish ritual was soon washed up and Pips were out of the question.

There was no discussion about evacuation. People just started leaving Middleburg as if politely drifting off from a party going wrong. They simply sought out quiet places, avoiding the restless movements of Earth. The Great Wobble, as it came to be called by Folk Science, which usurped the place of Western science, lasted a few weeks—much longer than the three-minute pole shift meteorologists had forecasted.

As things seemed to settle, people began to scout out the new world. They found that while things were pretty messed up and places were changed, Earth still offered some habitable areas. Middleburg was among them. Glacial erratics, aka dinosaur eggs, from the melting of the Ice Age, had rolled around again in the Great Wobble. They created a wall against the new sea that had risen where the Mississippi used to be. Trees had been tossed and had taken root in new places. Other places full of ferns and moss seemed untouched, as if the creature that had caused all this had been a giant unicorn. *A unicorn will not hurt a fern or crush any of the surrounding mosses because that is where the smaller fairy creatures live.*

Clearly things had shaken out well in Middleburg as compared to many places that were now under the Mississippi Sea. Many of their neighbors had gone back home, but Charles wanted to be sure the Wobble was really over.

When Charles was convinced that the Wobble was finished, he had asked Deb to marry him and live with him on his parents' land in Middleburg. Their daughter, Miranda, was all grown-up. This was not the first time he'd asked. On this occasion, he picked the right moment. Deb was in a lull. First her *Don't Blow It* series of travel guide shows had lost popularity, and then students started dropping out of her Creative World History classes after the first day. She had spent the last three years utterly alone. Miranda was far away. Socially and economically, Deb had lost her resources.

I still remember the conversation: OK, you be the man and I'll be the wife. Don't take it that way, Deb, you be the woman, I'll be your band. Like my group, I'd asked? Yes, we'll be a small group. Miranda too, she's in our group. It's natural, don't you see, Deb? Why did I avoid his hand for so long? Why has he been so persistent? Yes, let's go. Right now. To Middleburg, I'd said.

And so they had loaded up their backpacks and followed the paths to Middleburg, one of the few regions of tiny renaissance where survivors picked up their lives. There were many trails leading to Middleburg. Old neighbors came back, but there were newcomers too, people who just happened to be nearby when the Wobble came and heard that Middleburg was safe, and in its own way, booming.

In this post-world life, people often didn't live very long, and there were not many animals left. Remember when all the news used to be bad? We used to have headlines like, "Species going extinct at fastest rate since Ice Age," "Global warming renamed global chaos," and "Baby boomers deemed last healthy generation." Well, now the simple good news of continued life for our own and other species was rare, and it was all good news all the time. If we still had headlines, one might read, "Group of elderly women survive by helping each other and giving lectures on old-time skills."

For Deb and Charles, who were nearly elders, everything seemed late: they had intended to complete their cordwood house before the economy completely collapsed. Yet they were still building the house.

Charles was in his late teens when his parents, Thelma and Paul, planned it. They put in a well and the foundation, and had gathered many of the building materials. Back in 2004, Thelma, Paul, and young Charles had moved from their modern apartment to this land they had bought on the edge of town and began their preparations for the challenging world they saw coming, later exemplified by the financial mess of 2008, the BP oil spill and the earthquake and tsunami in Japan that damaged a nuclear plant. They decided they could live more simply, within their means, and close to nature. They erected a yurt on the land and lived happily in their glorified tent until a cyclone came and smashed the yurt, with Charles's parents crushed inside. It wasn't unusual to lose family members in those years of extreme storms, heat waves, heavy downpours, floods, cyclones, and droughts.

The weather systems were calmer now, though

not at all back to "usual." His parents had not expected to live through the great changes, but they did believe that if Charles was careful with his inheritance, he might make a life for himself.

Charles inherited the beginnings of a house. It was a strictly do-it-yourself project in a world without Home Depot. Deb remembered the predictions of global warming before the Wobble. Building projects went very fast then, boom, boom, boom. Until, suddenly off balance, Earth wobbled in a slow, rhythmic, unpredictable dance. Perhaps the end of time did not explain why the house remained incomplete. But life was slower, and things took more time.

Time had changed its stride. Certainly people did not experience the same old chronology—some vestige of it, yes, but also some letting go of time as a predictable machine-like presence.

People began to notice a sort of ten-year flextime. There was a dreamy subjectivity to time, and the reality of a person's age could be anywhere in the ten-year range. In other words, you would have to be dead for a full ten years before any chance of your also existing as alive was out of the question. If you thought you were forty years old, you could actually be thirty or fifty. The measurement of time was a lost science.

It was overwhelming to look at all that was left undone. The land cleared for their house was a mud pit. They were still cutting and splitting piles of wood that they had taken down two years before, just to get logs out of the way so they could have some space to work in what would be their yard. They were buried in firewood.

The neighborhood landmarks were scrambled, sometimes to their advantage. Though they had lost the yurt, they gained a small airplane hangar from a tiny rural airport that had scooched onto their land.

"I didn't plan on living in an airplane hangar all these years," Charles said, catching a dish towel Deb had tossed at him as he sat at the kitchen table, breakfast dishes pushed aside, looking over the blueprint his father had made.

"I'm just glad we found this place to live while we build our house. Seems like it came along just in time," Deb said.

"You're right about that. I was just saying I didn't plan on it. I intended on having a house built for you by now." He got up and drifted slowly over to Deb, draping her in his heavy arms of regret, but she slipped away.

"Sometimes, Charles, I don't even care. I'm as happy here as I'd be anywhere. I'm happy to be at the edge of the mountain, in the forest, in a quiet place. Maybe we don't need a special house for these 'apocalyptic times.' " She brought over a bucket of cold water to mix with the hot water from the rocket stove outside.

"You're wrong about that," Charles said. "Things are only going to get worse, we've just been lucky so far."

"I like luck a whole lot better than hard work," Deb said.

"Hard work helps me prove my father right about everything he said I'd be able to do. I may not be as smart and lucky as you, Deb, but I know how to work hard and I will build this house."

"Don't worry, Charles. We can do it together, just the way we've survived so far."

Deb said these things, but they never seemed very intimate to Charles. He knew she did not exactly belong to him. No matter how loyal he was, no matter how well he took care of her. They were like two train tracks, never crossing over into each other's space. Deb belonged to the land, to nature, to the Great Spirit. What really kept them together was this land: they each had their separate purposes on it. Charles worked it. Deb witnessed it. Charles brought use and survival from the land. Deb walked it, talked it, learned it, and loved it. Their world was not completely grim. There were many losses of species, yet the number of different flowers, mosses, and ferns Deb found walking the old mountain road was enough to fill her head and her heart.

Her calmness about the problems of the world and her own precarious situation in it came from an awakened thread in the blanketing consciousness of inevitable endings. This awakened thread was freedom. It sparkled with possibility in a dark gloomy picture, and colored everything. She had had a dream, back in the days when people were doing those things they might never have the opportunity to do again. Deb had returned home from a cruise with her extended family, seeing Europe and the Mediterranean Sea; it had been a great luxury to be able to do this. Yet as in all families, there had been tensions; there were days when they argued or came face-to-face with the ugliness of civilization. There were sicknesses and accidents. Mixed in there was euphoria, a good cup of coffee alone with her daughter. They all piled into a van and raced through towns and museums. So many experiences piled up, the good and the bad in a heap of colorful undigested clutter.

Undigested until a dream, which came to Deb some time after she returned to her home country. She dreamed she was back on the boat, on a long trip, and experienced everything from near starvation and eating her own shoes, to killing swordfish and getting infected, to stepping ashore and being treated like royalty.

Then one day, it was her last day, somehow her very last day ever. They were taking her to "her" island, where she would be dropped off and left alone. This may have been death. It was a beautiful morning. The sky was pretty, the air was balmy, and she had slept well. Everyone she met was kind and friendly; the cruise staff, her family, and many strangers gracefully milled about. There was a perfect and wonderful spirit to this, her last day. She felt honored. She could see her island in the distance. This feeling of complete satisfaction and wonder settled on her, reflecting backward over her entire past, purifying it. No longer were her experiences a heap of undigested castoffs. The spiritual light of this day spread in the most forgiving way to lift her entire life into supreme gratitude.

The gift of that dream affirmed her calmness in every storm and desperate time.

Deb worried that Charles might work himself to death like a worker bee in the summer, performing each task that needed to be done for the hive at different times of its life. According to old beekeeping books, summer bees lived four to six weeks, while winter bees could live four to five months. Summer bees lived only three weeks on average in more recent years, due to loss of food sources, chemical contamination, and disease outbreaks. Often she would stop him when he got "motorized." Not wanting to do something, Deb insisted, was a nudge from wisdom.

Perhaps they balanced each other, keeping the train on track. It wasn't a highly romantic kind of love. For Deb, it was almost impersonal. For

Charles, it just was what it was. Of course, love moved through phases, even if it never changed. Love moved beyond love, to a place where all that remained to sustain the relationship were the personal strengths of each.

It would have been better if they had finished building the house. Instead, they had the next best things: each other and their land in Middleburg, Vermont. It was forest now, as if the flat landing had just shifted off the map like obsolete postage. Prayer Mountain to the east had wobbled closer and edged out the landing field, no longer usable for aircraft. Lacking maintenance for many years, it had turned into woodland interspersed with mossy boulders.

For now they were living in the hangar, long abandoned by private jets. They found the motorcycle parked by the side door at the beginning of what seemed to be summer. Joe, a fan of Deb's travel guide series, left the motorcycle as a gift, and a way of sharing the story of Ruth, his late wife. Joe and Ruth used to travel together all over the country on their motorcycles. They had no children, just this one joy of being together on the road.

His eyes, Joe confessed, looked to every view through her. What was once an automatic togetherness was now a purposeful twining of his experience of the road with her memory. Without bringing her to mind, he couldn't travel; without traveling, he couldn't be himself. Joe was small, compact, fit, and bald. He seemed stoic about

Ruth's passing as if his loss only made things more as they were, more bitter and more sweet.

The mental picture of Ruth that came to Deb was happy. There were no actual photographs. *She appeared to have the same build as Joe but in female form. She had short wavy hair, and wore lipstick. But what really came through was culinary. Ruth was like bread. She could be a blueberry muffin or sourdough rye.*

Anyway, Joe couldn't use Ruth's motorcycle. Fuel was hard to come by, the motorcycle's mission was joy and it had a limited amount left to give. Deb and Charles shared the motorcycle with the community, loaning it out and shuttling people around. They only considered themselves caretakers of the Yamaha XT225 Serow. Deb maintained it, and Charles signed it out and kept track of its whereabouts. Only a thin remnant of a runway remained; they called it Ruth's Road for her motorcycle.

Charles had had some input on what sort of land his family would buy, and he wanted this place because it had plenty of trees for building and yet was close to the valley and flowers for the bees. Twenty years ago, Charles started a community roadside planting effort to help save the bees. The bees' favorite, white sweet clover, had spread everywhere there was open land.

It was a beautiful day in June and it felt surprisingly quite June-like. Such months had not been earning their reputations for many years. The resemblance to traditional seasons was slight.

Charles had spent his youth preparing for the end of the world, as they knew it. The prophecies of the native peoples seemed to speak to him directly, as if God himself had whispered his plans in Charles's ears. He didn't believe in God, though. He just believed in doing his best, and being neighborly. He saw no need for religion.

This morning was so pleasant they ate breakfast with the hangar doors wide open as well as two other windows, improvements they had made to their found dwelling. The breeze smelled like spring. Stacked on the left side of their one-room home were some freshly oiled and fabricated hive bodies they would use to catch honeybee swarms during the season, such as it was. The honey would keep them in sweets and give them something to trade for other items they needed. They also made candles from the beeswax and generally used the products of the hive as food, medicine, and currency.

Deb was sitting with her tea at her desk, sorting through her papers, seemingly lost in thought. Charles was gathering all the things he would need when he went beelining, hunting down feral hives in trees. Bait pads, scented syrup, stopwatch, notepad, compass, binoculars, smoker fuel, a hat, a rope, water and food, as well as a couple of hive bodies, were piled by the door. Outside the hangar, you could see they lived in building B1, as a square white sign above the door indicated, or "Bee one" as Charles liked to think of it.

"Deb?"

"Charles, give me some space. I'm onto something."

"What, analyzing ancient telephone doodles? I was hoping you would help me hunt down hives in the forest today."

Deb looked up from the notes she had taken while on the telephone with her grandmother, Grace, thirty years ago when they had phones, a yellowed newspaper scrawled in blue marker and decorated with doodles. These too, the newspaper and the Magic Marker, had become extinct.

"I will, but I don't feel ready yet. I'm wrangling a story right now."

"A Crisis Averted?"

"Yup, that's the one. Do you know what this story promises? Imagine a smooth and happy old age for yourself, and a peaceful time of prosperity on earth."

"How can a story change anything? And how do you find a story that may not even exist anyway? And why do you even try when there are so many things in real life that need to get done?"

"So many questions, thanks, I like that. Stories are the reason things are the way they are in the first place. The stories you tell yourself focus your life into something you can actually see. Once you see your life through the lens of a story, you are confined to the rules of that story, and the victories that can be achieved in such a context. For instance, the Fountain of Youth, that's a story. If you could find a person who had actually been to the Fountain of Youth, then you could go there too. That's how it works. I call it story wrangling because you have to wrestle with the truth that you want to come out of a situation. It's not a given. I'm not sure right now if I'm going to write the story or tell it. First, I have to find it."

"Very interesting. How did you start looking for this story of A Crisis Averted anyway?"

"I'm a peace-loving person, you know. So many stories are about how to resolve a crisis, but I just didn't want a crisis to happen at all, especially not to me, or my family. I want to be useful to the end of my days. I want to end suffering. I want to offer a new tool for happiness to humanity. I feel that there is a story I can discover, or a story-making process that will help people transform collective negative energy."

"Does this have anything to do with Grandpa Jim's story? Is that why you're reading old telephone notes from Grandma Grace?"

"Exactly so. I've got a hook in this story, deep in my Prozac-popping poppa, where no one would suspect it. Jim has carried his vocational crisis around like a ball and chain since they kicked him out of seminary for blowing his top seventy years ago. He's got A Crisis Averted and he doesn't even know it.

"In the very fact that I'm alive, I found the clue. We take everything for granted. That's why we can't see what's in plain sight. If any one of us could just be grateful that we are alive, A Crisis Averted would pop out of the background in the decaying leaves, and we would be blessed with a lightness of being in our old age, we would die without a single enemy. The earth we returned to would glow with gratitude that our life had been lived."

The whole time Deb was explaining this, her facial expression lit up and grew dark, contracted and expanded like the universe itself, and her hands moved as if she were dancing the words from the air. Her graying auburn hair was coming loose from a clip behind her ear, as if orderliness was deeply against the point she was trying to make.

"OK, Deb, I support you in this wrangling. Will you help me later this morning with the bees, and meet me out there?"

"Sure, I'll be at a stopping place with these notes soon. You go ahead."

Charles was eager to get going before the weather changed. Sometimes he was annoyed by Deb's delays, but when she took the time to explain her reasoning, he found himself grateful to have her in his life. Deb knew this sort of loyalty was rare and it pleased her.

He stood at the door with his stuff, observing the no-shoes-in-the-house rule. Deb went over and gave him a good-bye hug.

"Don't forget water," she said.

"Got it," he said.

While he loaded up his cargo bicycle outside, she arranged her desk, her tea, and a little bowl of hazelnuts to snack on. She just needed a little more time alone with the material. The observer's gaze developed the picture of truth.

CHAPTER 3

Deb briefly had a career story wrangling, as she now called it. She had been good at it in her day. She was not the type to push her luck, though, and what was luck worth when it was pushed anyway? She was like a desert: her flowering season came only with the infrequent rains. Somehow, it seemed less divine if you had to beg luck to stick around. Desert flowers need tenacious roots to remain viable for timeless dry spells, tough like burdock.

Her travel series, *Don't Blow It*, was a post-TV reality show. It was an interactive story with a set of characters that any participant could play. Towns competed to host the shows: they were transformed into settings for the half-God, half-human characters created by Deb and embodied by the populace to settle the earth's account. The stories changed the people who participated in the shows. By exposing the powerful God-side of themselves, they could be more fiercely authentic than ever before. For cross-marketing purposes, Deb had also created a series of travel guides to go with the site-specific reality plays. Very suddenly, the series lost popularity, and Deb started to dislike travel, competition, and interaction. You could tell by the light, which got real stingy, the time was no longer right for *Don't Blow It*. The series had generated a moment of admiration for Deb. One critic had called her "drop-dead modest." She was never sure how to take that. A moment of fame can be haunting.

She had been so many people in her life. She'd been the teenage mother, the famous reality writer, and the professor. She was now a wife and a sort of pioneer woman in a world very different than it was thirty years ago. Yet never before had she turned toward the vacuum that sucked her into being born in the first place. That seemed like a buffalo of a different color.

Turquoise blue. Who am I to interview the master of this animal? I have my own brown buffalo that I understand. It is frightening to look backward or forward in my lineage. Yet here I am, staring at the X on a treasure map, and the X is right on my heart. Digging, I find pieces of my ancestors, all mixed-up, hollow, and still calling me to earth to recreate what they started. Who is to say when something is finished?

Deb was done with all but enjoying the last of her life in a world that had frankly shifted more toward her liking. She liked primitive life: cooking over a campfire, not being bothered with phone calls, e-mail, and other electronic vibrations. She liked the small scale of humanity, the fact that there were fewer people. Yet the arrow had landed, pointing to the mystery, and the obligation of unfinished business.

The haunted feeling that arises is the clue that something is not finished, even in these bonus years. It is bubbling up from the past in delayed fermentation.

Looking at the telephone notes where Grace had answered her questions about the sad secret behind their lives, Deb compared her research into Granddaddy Jim's fall from a tall building and her imagining of this event, as retold by Grace. The truth had to be somewhere between the different versions. She refilled her tea from a tankard of hot water she had prepared over the fire the night before, as was her habit. The nuts were gone, and she began to pace and stretch to get fresh air into her system; this simple form of inspiration was part of her process. She believed in breathing.

Deb had been raised by her grandparents. Her real parents were too young to take care of her when she was born. Her mother, Helen, died in childbirth, and her father, Dezy, ran off with his banjo and never came back. Grace and Jim, Dezy's parents, had functioned as if they were her parents after that. Though her real parents obviously had unfortunate stories, life with Grace and Jim seemed uplifted from all misfortune, except when she found out about "The Crisis." Then a whole veil began to slowly unravel.

When she'd asked Jim more specific questions about the room and the general setting just prior to his suicide attempt, he gave a description much different than what she'd imagined. He was staying at the YMCA, training for a job with the Greyhound Bus Company. He was in bed, and slithered across the room. He didn't want to, but felt compelled to move toward the window. He thought of calling Grace on the phone. "But what could I say?" He squeezed himself between the louvers of the window and let go, screaming. He hit with great but "certainly not fatal force."

When you dig up the facts and try to clear away the mistaken way you have imagined things, it seems sometimes that you have traded gold for silver. I always imagine my Jim/dad sitting at a grand desk when the compulsion to jump from the high-rise hit him. He was not the owner of the desk. The authority figure (God? the psychiatrist? the boss?) had stepped out of the room momentarily. Jim took the opportunity to usurp his position, sitting on a powder keg behind the desk. The desk, feeling its master was being betrayed, shot a terrible force of thought into Jim. It was a mind control ejector seat. The compulsion was the ammo the magic desk used to reclaim itself for its true master. Before the authority figure reentered the room, Jim was propelled by a thought wave to jump out the window. I have always imagined it in a somewhat comical light like that.

The light was changing, and Deb felt her own chair give her a little shock as if saying it was time to get up, and get out. Yes, time was passing, and she had promised to meet up with Charles to help him with whatever situation turned up with the bees. Deb generally found the bees to be more unpredictable than did Charles, who always seemed to have a plan for them. She would go on a pollen walk, she decided, on the way to the place where she knew Charles would be, the same tree where they had suspected bees were living. It was not because of any evidence from beelining, but just a sort of intuition, perhaps wishful thinking about the tree. Or thinking, *if I were a bee, that's where I would go.*

A pollen walk, Deb called it, when she went to take pollen from a drawer they had installed at the bottom of one of their beehives. She imagined walking on a path of velvet pollen pearls. The bees shaped each tiny ball from flower dusts in shades of yellow, orange, brown, and purple, somehow royal in their velvet way. In her mind's eye, those colors were her spiritual path on these walks, but first she had to get dressed. She was still in her nightshirt, which had pictures of pink cupcakes all over it. She switched to an orange T-shirt and white painter's pants.

She started out down Ruth's Road until she got to the path. There weren't so many now, but people still kept up the roads in the neighborhood. It made things seem more neighborhoody, like what they remembered from childhood before the end of oil. For longer distances, those who could flew a magic carpet infused with universal life energy.

Carpet-pools were arranged with people who had magic carpet abilities as not everyone did. The world was no longer car-centered, and this left more space around buildings. Deb preferred to walk even for somewhat longer distances, drumming the ground and moving in a self-healing way. The feeling of traveling by magic carpet was very much like zooming in a car. The lone motorcycle they had was a relic, a nostalgic toy. No one needed it, but it had sentimental value and was a fun addition to life. Bicycles, especially cargo bicycles, were very common. Walking was slower and allowed Deb to notice things.

Suddenly, out of the blue, her thoughts stopped short. She almost walked right into a baby woodchuck.

"Hello, little creature. What are you doing here?"

The animal, long, furry, and fat with inquisitive button eyes, just sat there looking at her. Deb didn't know what else to do or say, so she started to take a step forward, to continue on her way. At this, the creature darted into a cave-like space between some rocks. Then another creature just like the first except larger came out and made a strange noise at her, a sort of scolding, coughing sound. How strange. Yet it seemed to Deb that this kind of thing was happening often. Yesterday on a walk, she had had the same kind of encounter with a baby squirrel. *It's as if a rumor is going around about me.* The day before yesterday, a thin black cat followed her, screaming like a crow, its tail up and slanted forward, ears back. By running just ahead of her, the cat forced her to follow. The cat seemed to be warning her about some unseen predicament. Cats can see an enemy in a speck of dust.

As Deb neared the beeyard, she picked some flowers to give to the bees as a token of her appreciation for the pollen that she was about to collect. A cartoon image of a rain cloud flashed across her mind. She remembered seeing the image in dream mail. She looked up and saw gray shifty clouds, but ignored the warning. When she arrived at the hive and pulled out the drawer, she discovered only a teaspoon of pollen. She tasted a pinch. The wisdom of the flowers is very healthy food, high in protein and B vitamins. Now that she thought about it, there was no need to collect pollen, since the bees didn't fly in the rain and therefore didn't gather pollen. All the bees were flying back into the hive now. The rain was coming soon. The bees knew. They lined up at the hive entrance and filed in one by one.

Once the bees were safe inside the hive, the rain came, and Deb ran. She thought she might stay drier that way, but it was hopeless: her orange T-shirt wet and clingy, the knees of her pants sticking to her legs. At least it wasn't cold, and the pollen was safe in a birch-bark pouch. As she ducked into the forest to get out of the rain, she saw a blue light dash from her right. It leaped toward her out of the trees like a jungle cat. It seemed to go right through her and vanish into her head.

What could it be? Some sort of reflection? Rain on my glasses? I simply thank it for showing up. I've gotten into the habit of just saying thanks. So much of what we mistake for a threat is actually benevolence.

That much she knew as she attempted her unique path to wrangle stories for the service of humanity: One wrestled with angels, not demons. The truth of the golden harp could be learned only from an angel, and angels were often tough. Who were the guardians of the truth she sought? Every being she met in her quest must have ownership in the story she sought. Love and respect, that was the ticket onto the battleground of story wrangling. By the time the forest path ended, she was back on the road and the sun was shining again.

She found Charles in a tree with a swarm. This was great luck, even better than finding a feral hive in a tree, because a swarm is ready to move into a new home. The swarm was in a ball around a limb just above Charles's head. He had a box ready below them, but not enough hands to hold the box, shake the bees off the limb, and stay in the tree all at the same time. Deb, still damp from her microclimate experience, climbed up and gave the branch a thump. The bees fell into the box and their queen with them, apparently, since they re-congregated happily in there. Honeybees will always stay with their queen when swarming. Straggler bees that weren't caught flew in to be with her. Charles closed up the hive entrance, and loaded it onto the cargo bike. They went home, Charles on the bike and Deb by foot.

At home, they pumped water and carried buckets of it back to the airplane hangar. Deb made a fire, and Charles put together some dried mushrooms, leeks, and beans for a soup.

"Thanks for your help today," Charles said.

"I'm sorry I didn't help that much, but I'm so happy we have a hive at home now," Deb said.

Deb brought out some mead she had made last year with unripened honey and wild grapes.

"Cheers," she said, filling their glasses.

"We'll have to protect them," Charles said.

"Why? There are no bears."

"I don't know. There should be bears. There have always been bears. I've always protected my hives."

"Maybe we could make a place for them inside so they can fly in and out?" Deb suggested.

"Maybe. Maybe that's a good idea."

They were both tired and let it rest there. Maybe they would keep them like pets, inside. Deb sort of liked the idea. It was a sweet and warming thought, and she felt chilled from the night air and being wet. Often she craved chocolate. She felt thin and strong like an animal that didn't need candy. But she still craved the foreign intensity of chocolate and feared some sort of caloric debt that would weaken her.

They were quiet now and ate their soup with acorn bread. Their food was good and satisfying, but never more than enough. The honey from the bees and the mead Deb made were luxuries. Meat was out of the question. Deb hadn't smelled a barbecue in the neighborhood since childhood. A combination of factors had conspired to make vegetarians out of everyone: loss of habitat, fewer animals, changing sensibilities, animal rights activists, hunters failing to mentor new hunters, animal husbandry lost to industrial farming, and industrial farming failing like every other industry too big to fail.

"I hope this isn't the last bottle. We'll need some for Ermal, he's going to help us raise the rafters on our house. Anyway, it's good to have extra around to trade. Some people like mead better than honey," Charles said.

"I put half the bottles in a separate box for bartering, and I doubled the batch. We have a lot to do this year, and we'll need every kind of currency we can conjure," Deb said.

"We have to make more beeswax ingots soon."

"I'm working on a new mold that will tell our story. And I need a cool day to melt the wax down."

They put a big pot of water on the fire for washing dishes. It was Deb's turn, and she was glad there weren't too many tonight. It often took an hour or more to wash dishes, and she wanted to get back to her research.

Perhaps this slow life with all its chores and lack of modern convenience was a more natural vocation than the sort of career Jim/dad had searched for. Yet Deb did not find the answer to vocation in her homesteading lifestyle any more than Jim/dad had been satisfied with working at Pic-a-Pack. The answer was not "in" anything. The answer was suffused into everything she did.

God is with me in all that I do. That was the humble way, the way of a person with displaced gifts. A Crisis Averted does not need anyone's recognition as a legitimate vocation.

She could empathize with Jim/dad. It was hard to be humble and great, somebody and nobody, special and ordinary at the same time. It was hard not to give up one realization for the other.

Back at her desk in her pajamas, sitting with her legs thrown over the arm of her chair as if sitting in a basket, she meditated on Jim's story, sent it up to her third eye, everything she knew about it. She was convinced that somewhere in that story was a gem, a real treasure that would especially shine when she brought it out herself. She physically dissolved any complication. She was slippery and nothing could attach itself to her. She was a reed through which all things became reduced to essential form. Except things she had never noticed. That was why she must look very carefully at this history that somehow was never digested into its highest form.

Immaturity makes honor more expensive than it needs to be. The samurai falls on his sword. Jim jumps out a window. A janitor a few floors below was cleaning windows; as he opened the window outward to clean it, my grandfather crashed through it. If the janitor had not broken his fall, Jim would be dead, and my father never would have been born, and then neither would I have been born. Jim told me that if I became a teacher, "The most important person to befriend is the janitor. The janitor has the power to make things difficult or easy for you depending on if he likes you." Jim suffered a severe break in his arm and also broke his back in the fall. He was flat on his back for quite a while.

Deb's grandfather, less than ten years dead, still appeared healthy, and you would never have known that he had once had a broken back and a badly broken arm. He never complained of pain. He never got sick. Deb first learned of his suicide attempt when she was sixteen and leaving home "to find her fortune." Though really it was some weird maternal fever that compelled her to get away from everyone when she unexpectedly became pregnant.

Before leaving home, she decided to take a look at Jim's palm to see if she might learn anything about him that had been hidden all these years. She noticed a scar and asked him about it. He told her he had gotten it from crashing through the glass window. He was sitting alone in a room at the YMCA and felt a compulsion to jump out the window. He was angry with God. He just jumped. But when she first heard this story, she didn't think of it as a suicide attempt.

Her thoughts seemed to make her invisible in one world and visible in another, like an animal in the forest seen only by its own kind. Her hair changed color. Her skin was transparent. She was delicate and flitting like a deer. Chipmunks came close to the window and lay about as if it was story time.

When she first recognized her calling to find a story that would aid all humanity in old age, and bring peace and prosperity on earth, she decided to call Jim's act what it was: a suicide attempt. She changed the language of her inquiry, in a sly effort to get Jim to be more grown-up about his actions. He had to have known that the fall could have killed him and that he would have left his wife a widow, and Deb's father fatherless. (Not to mention that Deb herself would never have been born.) He might have been blinded by his anger, but he had to admit it was a suicide attempt.

It was 1963 when Grace received the news via the front page of a newspaper with a picture of Jim face down at the bottom of the YMCA building. Apparently, this was not a newspaper the family kept. Deb never asked to see it, although she'd seen it in her mind many times.

It happened while Jim was away in Memphis, Tennessee, where he was training to be a Greyhound bus dispatcher after he gave up on becoming a minister. Grace and baby were staying with her parents in Houma, Louisiana, when she got the call from Jim saying, "I want to talk." Grace left the baby with her mother and took the bus to Memphis. This guy got on the bus when they pulled into Memphis and wanted to know, "Who is Grace Exlander?" Grace, sensing that it was bad news, just said, "I have to go to the bathroom." When she came out, the man showed her the newspaper.

In secluded sorrow, Grace and Jim stood by each other.

Unlike Dezy's X generation, with no secrecy, no shame, only ambition, claiming, "No one will drag me down," Grace humbly looked after Jim. He was on his back for many months. She changed his bedpan. She kept him company while he watched *You Bet Your Life*. Jim loved to laugh at how abusive Groucho Marx could be, how he could say anything no matter how rude, irreverent things that Jim would never say. Great healing laughter came while watching Groucho. Having that one thing to look forward to may have kept Jim alive.

Grace had always been very practical about well-being. Deb heard in her mind's ear Grace saying, "Get some rest." Charles was asleep and Deb quietly bedded down beside him.

In the morning, after she woke up, Jim's last

description of his fall seemed to have evolved overnight. Deb imagined slithering out of bed to fulfill her mission, just like Jim/dad. She told Charles, who was reading beside her,

"I'm going to slither out of bed and take a shower now."

I feel sort of lizard-like, sneaky and half-ashamed of what I am now going to do. In the half-light of morning I'm half-lizard, half-zombie. Only my arms can move, the rest of me follows.

Once she was out the front door, the zombie-lizard feeling evaporated in the pink morning sun. Their outdoor solar shower consisted of a water bag hanging from between two trees, with a tube ending in a dangling showerhead. She stood on the wooden pallet under it, pulled the spigot open, and awakened to the humorous contrast between dreams and life. They lived in such a down-to-earth way. Even the tall rock standing by the shower had a natural indentation they used for soap, and in this indentation, a small, cute tuft of grass that looked just like a fluffy little scrubby brush had decided to grow. The zombie-lizard remnants of her dream seemed beyond recall.

CHAPTER 4

At nineteen, Deb reenacted Jim's jump from a high-rise. It happened on a travel-writing gig in San Francisco, where the apartment she stayed in was on the third floor. When she saw the private depth from her window, she was tempted to try her father's self-destructive compulsion. She wanted to see what it was like to throw herself over the edge. Imitation was a strategy often seen in nature, so it must really work. The couch in the courtyard below was part of the inspiration. She wanted to do a stunt; she didn't plan to get hurt. She had been taking photographs of garbage seen from great heights in forgotten areas between buildings. It would be like entering the photograph.

She talked about the jump with her editor first, and her editor advised against it. He did not vigorously dispute Deb's idea that it was possible to jump without getting hurt, though. She felt she could do it, so she leaped out the third-story window and landed successfully on the couch in the courtyard.

She still had the travel piece about the tall

apartment buildings of San Francisco. She included her window-jumping adventure in the original version:

"The couch pillows were pretty springy, and there was no feeling of 'great force' as Grandpa Jim had told me he had felt upon landing in 1963. The most amazing thing about it was how quickly it was over and the contrast of time and effort it took to climb back up, via the metal fire escape."

Now, as Deb reread her words, she was struck by the one similarity between his jump and hers: the lack of consideration for others. What if her jump had been unsuccessful? What a bummer it would have been for her editor and roommate at the time—her good friend, truth be told—if she had ended up badly hurt or dead? And what about her grandparents, Grace and Jim? What about her daughter? Would she have been born anyway, or was Deb her only conduit into this world? Why had she not considered these things?

A painful shard of blame lodged in Deb's back for a few days, the sad story weighing on her, though she tried to ignore it. *My aches are not so bad that I can't disguise them.* Grace had taught her that toughness was a virtue, and she absorbed this value readily. Over these blame-stabbed days, her thoughts turned to other times in her life when she had fallen, failed, gotten hurt and survived, just like Jim had fallen, failed, gotten hurt and survived. Perhaps her life was a series of reenactments. Though

Charles was her first love, he was her third husband, and Deb had had her share of picking up pieces. She knew what it meant to survive disaster. She had lived through a time not only of personal disasters but also of catastrophic weather that changed the world she lived in.

Her mind turned now to the part in her story about the time and effort it took to climb back up. Feeling her own pain, and Jim's pain, she began to feel something else: a light feeling that made her get up and understand that she had a second chance, and that it was very precious. She had her experience, her learning, and also her life to live anew. There were scars, and echoes of abandonment all through her family, but a life saved from waste was precious, especially to the descendants.

Loss was Deb's greatest frustration. She brought Loss with her from the spirit world, a light from the past into the future. Losing a sock was as maddening as losing a species. To compensate, she became good at finding things and put herself at the service of anyone who was looking for something. She had a hawk's eye. Empathy amplified the desire to help into a mission to find the lost things of humanity.

Cities like San Francisco still stood but in a modified way, with fewer tall buildings, with fewer buildings all told, as if they had gone back in time or tried to morph back into small towns. Not everyone lived as simply as Deb and Charles, but most lived more naturally and modestly than they did before the Great Wobble. The tall buildings had become a different sort of tourist attraction. People liked to go up on the top floors and meditate. Some said these buildings brought them closer to God, reaching for the skies as they did. Deb knew that trees, though not as tall, were better for this, because they were alive and rooted deep in the ground. She didn't mention that at the time of her travel piece, though; she didn't want to pop the balloon of longing people had for these remnants, and for restoration.

They had used donkeys in the city, she remembered, to carry groceries home from the market. She wondered if you could still get a donkey anywhere. Wouldn't it be fun to walk with a donkey carrying your supplies on his back? The idea of being friends with your transportation was appealing to Deb. There used to be a farm nearby that sold donkeys. She and Charles had visited once in another lifetime, so to speak. At Ass-pirin Acres, there had been all kinds of adorable donkeys, some of them still with their baby fur. There was one very sweetly shaped black one named Sparky, she remembered, wondering if somewhere, somehow, she might still find a donkey. She had been too shy to touch the furry animals, though she wanted to. She remembered how Charles had held her hand and reached out to stroke the nose of the donkey nearest to them.

Extinctions, declining numbers in all species, and a less human-dominated world meant that domesticated animals were not the norm. Humans were often without animal companions, animal services, and animal products. This was not a time of abundance.

That night, Deb couldn't sleep until she shared her wish to get a donkey. She turned to Charles just before he fell asleep, and asked:

"Oh Charlie-warley, will you be my donkey, like Sparky at Ass-pirin Acres, remember?"

"Yes, Deb, I think it might be better that way. I don't think a real donkey would be so easy to find."

"It'll be fun, Charles. Think of the places we'll go. We'll ride into town and you can carry supplies on your back. We can go up into the mountains for a picnic."

"Sounds like fun. I could make a little cart for you to pull."

"No, you be the donkey, I'll be your human."

"Will you scratch me behind the ears and give me carrots?"

"Yes, I'll spoil you rotten. All you have to do is look cute and help me pull my load."

"I don't want you comparing me to Sparky. He was cute because he was a baby when we saw him, remember? That's not fair. You can't compare a baby donkey to an old man."

"No, I'll love you for you, just the way you are."

"As a donkey?"

"Sure."

One mind manipulated the world, while the other received and transmitted waves of a dream. Deb was emotional about the weather lately, especially at night. The Egyptians once believed that the pharaoh's emotions caused the weather. Today's sudden rainstorm pierced Deb with a feeling of responsibility. As if one raindrop of her feelings could be the tipping point for a major flood.

Last night she saw a light, perhaps a moonbeam dancing. There was only half a moon last night and some lightning. She was in bed, resting in her husband's arms, when a light appeared over his shoulder.

She silently told the light:

I don't always feel so peaceful in this matrimonial snuggle, sometimes I love solitude too much. I seek something in solitude so intently that intimacy distracts and irritates each cell of my body. Tonight I'm completely relaxed and at home . . . how strange, how nice.

In the morning, Deb slipped out of bed early

and wrote a report of the incident:

I've noticed that light and color seem to respond to my feelings, even my breathing. I was lying there at peace, looking over his shoulder at a light that appeared. He was starting to fall asleep so I didn't mention the light, but it seemed special. As I relaxed into the feeling of the light, it brightened and changed, making me ooh and ah, as if this were more than an embrace. There were tears streaming down my face but no sadness. I couldn't take my eyes off the light. It danced. It sharpened into a tiny dot. A golden rod, and then it shifted into a ribbon dance. Sometimes it was blue, then gold, then white.

Who is the light? I have often found myself wondering this about certain light forms that appear. Light comes from the sun and falls here and there. We don't name individual pieces of it and say that they have independent identities, or personalities. The same goes for shadows. Yet sometimes a light seems to act in a certain way that provokes me to ask, "Who are you? Tell me about yourself." I interact with light as if it had a personality. I breathe the light in and out. I let it be. I am a scientific lunatic who notices things. I catch reflections that let me see things not ordinarily within range. I'm hyperaware of movement.

Once I saw such a light dancing in a field and found a witness to see it with me. The witness saw a sign that read "Safety Zone" and explained to me that the light was just moonlight flashing on the sign. I don't think the witness saw the magical dance of light that I saw, and I didn't see the actual sign until I walked right up to it.

I couldn't take my eyes off the light that appeared to me in our room last night. I was convinced that it was special, clearly a light of blessing. When I opened my heart to it, I was rewarded with a moving performance. When I doubted it was really there, it dimmed and became less interesting.

I couldn't take my eyes off it and I couldn't sleep. Incredibly relaxed, I was vibrating to the story of creation, a lullaby that keeps you from scratching while the weeds come up.

An old and stupid argument was keeping me awake: Is human birth less miraculous because you know how it happens?

Maybe the light from earlier in the day just never died. I had lit a candle in the morning as a vigil for the ocean and the creatures that still survive at unknown depths. Somehow believing that Jacques Cousteau's dream could bring back ancient forms to dazzle us with their beauty once again. I forgot to blow out my candle burning with love, devotion, and healing for so many crimes against the sea. I left for the day and did not remember it till I returned.

That candle by rights should have been used up. There was so little wick left, yet it burned on. I remembered the still-burning candle as I was traveling by magic carpet to visit my friend Irene, but I didn't worry because the candle is set up to be safe when unattended. Maybe the light of the candle stayed in the room.

The weather was odd yesterday, pleasant, then stormy, rain and hail, back and forth like that. On my way home, storm clouds raced after me. It was so dark when the clouds overtook me, it was as if three hours had passed in the blot of a shadow. Yet I could see morning-glory blue on the other side of the sky.

My attention was completely taken with flying the carpet as carefully as I could. Mental state is very important in controlling a flying carpet: you must be alert and at peace because the steering wheel is in your heart. I couldn't lose track of the fey-lines or the carpet would stop in the air, going nowhere. The rain and the fact that I was scared made it hard to see clearly, but at least I was dry. Even a lost art can be found and improved with a bit of faith. Long, long ago, the art of weaving and specially dying flying carpets was forbidden. Recipes, carpets, and artisans were burned. They didn't have the invisible bubble protecting the carpet back then, the "Devil-inspired contraption" as early Muslim rulers called the carpets. The artisans, madmen, and thieves who created and used these carpets in ancient history were a threat to the economic establishment then based on horses and camels. It was the same story with the electric car: a threat to the auto and oil industries. In a shattered economy, creative recovery is again possible.

I noticed a bright double rainbow against the gray residue of the storm. I flew right through one end of it twice. I remembered everything they say about the end of the rainbow and I was feeling quite fortunate. "I am receiving the rainbow light," I told myself. The particles of different-colored hadrons were all over me, like rice at a wedding party.

You experience light or a rainbow a certain way because of where you are standing. It's all about the angle. That's something I heard. I don't believe it. The determining factor in witnessing light is not only where you are standing, at which angle to the sun, but on a deeper level—what your relationship is with this light, and the source from which it comes.

In the dark, I see a light so affirming. I say to myself, all light is sacred. And maybe the darkness is sacred too.

Deb wrote to the sound of Charles sweeping the floor with a natural-bristle broom, made from sorghum they had grown. It was the most beautiful sound to write to, cleansing and calming, like having your hair combed, and as regular as ocean waves crashing to shore. Nothing made Deb feel more loved than when Charles did the housework.

∾ CHAPTER 5 ∾

Though time did not always move sequentially, people still had a sense of when their birthday was approaching. The exact day was not known, so it was customary to celebrate when the signs and signals of one's birth month seemed apparent. Deb felt the June-ness of June even without lilacs. Something still came around that felt fresh and new like the beginning of summer. Charles surmised Deb's birthday was near, and he wanted to do something special, but unfortunately he had to work for Ermal.

Ermal had helped Charles's parents transition to a simpler life on the land, and whenever Charles and Deb needed someone to help, like with putting up the rafters for their house, Ermal was the most reliable person. He always showed up. Often with his own crazy ideas about how things should go. Ermal often talked about Atlantis, how they did it such and such way and it worked there, so that was how we should do it here. It was too ridiculous, too far beyond anything that Charles believed. Atlantis! Even if he did believe in it, Atlantis was under water! Why should we do anything like they did?

The weird thing was, Deb observed, Ermal usually had a point; there was a rational kernel in all his suggestions. Much of what they had achieved would not have been possible without him; there was only so much two people could do by themselves. He had helped his parents put up the yurt. He also advised them to create their own composting humanure toilet system, which Deb and Charles still used today. Ermal seemed like a crazy old uncle. Charles wasn't related to Ermal, but they had known each other a long time.

Ermal looked like a rail but worked like a horse, a smart horse. He was getting older and spoke of injuries and feeling worn. Still, Ermal was one of the best men you could have around if you needed a helping hand.

Deb's birthday had sentimental significance, but working for Ermal had practical implications. Social capital had become more important since the whole idea of currency washed away. It was not as if they could just hire professional help like in the old days, even if they had been rich.

Rich people had to remake themselves with other means of power. Consciousness was changing. Check? Cash? Card? Plastic? Gold? PIN? Password? It came to pass that any question about currency generated a blank stare. Once you got the blank stare, you lost access to your currency simply by forgetting how to access it. It was like forgetting where you parked your car in the mega lots of the old days. Some people recovered and remembered their passwords, but this was often temporary, and no one felt certain that they would ever be able to use their money. Getting cash from a machine was a fluke. Even if they could get the money, who would take it? Sometimes people did take it, but this too was a fluke.

Most people had forgotten if they were rich or poor in their past lives. Sometimes it was just an itchy feeling in the back pocket or a distracting dollar sign in the back of the head; phantoms of an old persona that was "well-off" or "wealthy."

Sharing became the new transaction. Bartering. Friending. Liking. Trading. TimeBank. Favorpals. MiddleburgBucks. YesterDollars. These words filled in the gaps as chunks of forgetting entered the marketplace. Currency consciousness was changing like a collage: sections of the picture would fall out and be replaced with another section that seemed to fit, yet was quite different and surreal.

"What can I get money for?" changed to, "Do you like me, and do you have what I need?" See how the replacement section fits with the old dialogue, but it's different? A secret garden had been placed in public, right on the cold cement of the bank. The iron bars of the neighborhood were warmer now, more decorative than forbidding.

Reflected moonlight from the washbowl water

projected onto the dark ceiling in a perfect circle of light, trembling in tiny concentric waves as they watched.

"That is a very cool thing to see," Charles said, jiggling the water to watch its effect on the "screen" above their heads.

Deb had been awake for hours, drinking tea, remembering dreams, and writing by candlelight. Charles had been sleeping off and on, worrying about everything he didn't have time to worry about during the day. When sunrise poked through the high window above him, he got up, dressed, went to the bathroom, and washed his hands and face.

"It looks like I may be away helping Ermal during your birthday week, Deb, but I'll leave you the karma card. Go into town and have an old-fashioned shopping spree, within reason of course."

"How old will I be, anyway?" Deb wondered out loud.

"You're fifty-three, but that's not the point. The point is you're here now. That's something to celebrate."

"Thanks. I have no idea how I'm going to use the karma card yet."

"Use it to get closer to your story if you can, or just enjoy your birthday week."

"OK."

Deb kept a box of wishes under the bookshelf, in an old cigar box. She had been keeping it for about fifteen years. She didn't add to it often, but enjoyed assembling a collection that could be enjoyed for its own sake. She decided to put the karma card in there till she was ready to use it. When she opened the box, a piece of paper she had never noticed before came gliding out, a folded white square exactly the same size of the karma card itself. She opened it and read: *I don't want to live a life filled with manual labor.*

"Ha," she sighed with a deflated laugh. Well, too late for that. She crumpled it and tossed it in the fire where Charles was making oatmeal.

"What's that?"

"Just cleaning out some papers."

"I hope you don't have any more while I'm cooking. The ashes fly up and get in the food when I lift the lid."

"No more for now," she said.

Her eye caught a pink piece of paper floating on top of the others. One word, *piano*, was written upon it. Deb barely remembered what a piano sounded or looked like. She imagined it as a toothless whale. One would go inside to strum and play a song from the baleen—what the whale has instead of teeth to filter krill from the sea. No, a piano was supposed to go in the living room; it lived there like a musical desk that anyone who could play was free to use. It meant you were someone with the resources to do more than just survive. Gray hair and wrinkles had changed her image, giving gravity to her womanhood, and she wondered if it was too late to be someone who did more than just survive. She was not going to become a piano player now. A piano was too big, cumbersome, and altogether too fine a piece of furniture to have in her life.

The search for A Crisis Averted is not going to be the kind of thing where I can lug a piano along with me.

Birthdays seemed to come like popcorn popping. Deb's daughter and mother both had birthdays in June. It was like a contagious disease, this infatuation with June. *Lilacs, roses, peonies, what's not to like about June?* Sweet smells, balmy cool nights, and the beginning of long summer days. That was what everyone thought of even if you really couldn't expect anything so consistent anymore when it came to seasons.

Deb felt her bump on the wheel was coming: the place where her daughter entered, a reminder of her mother and where she came from. How old was she? At least fifty. Charles had said fifty-three, but she wasn't sure she was that old. She knew that her life as a mother was over and the end of her life was somewhere around the bend. Or was it? Was it a long ending? Longevity generally ran in her family, excepting her mother. One just never knew where one stood in relation to dying. *The shape of life, the phases of life, what happens after motherhood, is also without an exact formula. A little extra padding on her belly and breasts: Is that how the shaper adorned and signified her as an older woman?*

61

The karma card reminded Deb of one of the first birthday parties she ever attended. One of the gifts was a stuffed wiener dog made of white cotton cloth on which everyone signed birthday wishes. The karma card was sort of like that: If you did something that could be considered a community service, someone would usually notice and sign your karma card. The value was subjective. Often someone would give you a higher exchange if they recognized a signature and it meant something to them, or if the look of the card was impressive. Deb and Charles shared a card, as was common with couples, and theirs looked very impressive. Deb encouraged signers to use color, and Charles was active in community projects, like path maintenance, gleaning, and disaster cleanup.

Barter was also used, and Deb planned to meet with a group of ladies in their seventies, maybe even eighties, who dubbed themselves the Lecturing Ladies. They had a sort of end-of-the-world survivors club. It was doing very well, economically and spiritually. It seemed to be one of the few businesses holding together right now. Deb was their market research person. She gathered information about possible venues and topics of interest for the Lecturing Ladies.

These women were old because they were born before the chemical and genetic assault on food got really bad. People born after the 1990s didn't get that old. These Lecturing Ladies had survived and figured out a way to keep surviving. They took care of each other. They lived together in groups of three to four per house. A member of each house called the other houses each day, monitoring each other constantly with communication stones. For YesterDollars they lectured and taught old-time skills and nearly lost arts. Deb created a list of people interested in hearing about the planets and how they affected our lives. She located a comfortable barn and a pizza parlor as no-cost options for the lecture. The old ladies took it from there. Deb didn't really see herself becoming one of the old ladies. Maybe she already was a charter member and didn't recognize it. She was born before the 1990s, but she was not sure it was long enough before.

They promised her two pairs of knitted slippers with leather soles stitched on the bottom for her and Charles. Compensation came at irregular times, but it always came eventually, and provided the most useful things. She was lucky to have this connection to the grandmothers.

While Charles was gone, she used the karma card to get a haircut. It had been years since she had been to A Haircut Supreme. She asked for the newest and therefore least expensive stylist. His name was Shawn, and he was showing her all the new things they had to offer since she was there last. She could have a mud bath in the mudroom, or sit in the coloring café. She could watch the artful fountain flow with relaxing music and light, or get a spiritual reading from the crystal ball.

Deb peeked in the room. It was dark except for the truth stone, which was not a ball exactly, but more of a glowing egg.

"Oh!" Deb said. "How much extra is that?" She didn't want to deduct so many signatures that the karma card would look blank when she gave it back to Charles.

"Nothing extra," Shawn said and led her into the room, where he sat on one side of the mysterious rock and she sat on the other. He didn't even look at the crystal ball, just opened his hands to it, as if to receive its message through his hands, and closed his eyes.

"Did you know you have a great light bursting from your solar plexus? You have a lot of creative work to do—what's holding you back? Your spirit needs you to do this work or—and I don't want to threaten you, but you could get sick or even die if you don't get busy on this. You need to focus on it, stop being distracted. I see your father near this project. Is he a publisher? I see a publisher who is very fond of you. You just need to do the work, put in the time, and write the book. I could tell you more but the spirit has spoken, nothing else is important."

"My father is a banjo player; he ran off the day I was born. My publisher fell ill and died many years ago. I was a writer, that's what I used to do. I thought maybe I would just tell the story this time. Who bothers with the written word anymore?"

Was the truth stone referring to a book she had already written or to one she was going to write? Was writing as an art form completely passé? Dream mail was a common way to share ideas now. Souls could go into a slumber and telepathically send images and more; a good dream mailer could send all kinds of sensations as well. The College on the Hill hoarded books in a sort of museum. Theoretically, they could be checked out, but most people came just to look at them and read the titles. Books in homes were very uncommon. The only people Deb knew with books in their homes, except herself, were the Lecturing Ladies. People could read and write in English and a few other languages, but literature as an art form had suffered cultural displacement. Shawn had complete faith in the spirits, and clearly they said "book," and anyway Shawn said, "Books are still revered if not often used."

Deb thought the spirits might be referring to her story wrangling, rather than an actual book. Shawn seemed to move in and out of channeling the spirit, sometimes talking with the authority of spirit and sometimes putting in his own two cents on the matter. Deb was unsure which was more valuable. "When you use words in written form, you are dealing with something real, and collaborating with a higher source. When I cut your hair, I collaborate with your God-given looks and change your appearance. I don't just cut the air and leave you looking the same as when you walked in. Writing is much more effective than babbling if you're searching for some evidence, or want to leave some."

Shawn seemed very practical, like a nurse, insisting Deb's husband must be managed so that the proper care would be given to Deb's "book," aka her healing process. He gave strict instructions on how to deal with Charles if she found him to be an impediment to her work.

"I know Charles," he said. "He has a lot of things going on, a real busy body. But that doesn't mean you have to be. A writer needs meditative space. And I can tell by your hair that you are easily distracted."

Deb tried to remember Shawn's words; they were like ammunition to her. She was easily distracted, and Charles's activities did seem more practical and therefore more important to her. She often kept her own work secret, now that her stardom had ended.

Finally, Deb said, "That's what I came for, a less distracting haircut, something neat and sleek."

"OK," Shawn said. "Let's wash your hair."

He led her to a row of black cushiony reclining chairs, with black sinks behind them. She leaned back and closed her eyes. Shawn started massaging her head with shampoo. As the warm soapy water flowed through her hair, Deb had a dream. She took her pig for a walk on a bridge. The pig was not well trained and pulled on his leash, dragging her around. Maybe I should have trained him to walk like a dog, but then again she thought: *He is not a dog. He is an adorable pig, snorting along, expressing his pig-ness.* Then he fell off the bridge. Deb still had him by the leash and tried to pull him up. But he did not like this pressure and snorted in protest. So she lowered him back down, and then his leash fell off. Deb felt a sense of danger now with her pig on the loose.

Deb awoke, realizing that she had been snorting out loud. Sleeping, snorting, whatever the client did during a session was normal to Shawn. It was supposed to be a relaxing experience for the client, and he had been trained to allow whatever might happen in such a state.

He led her to his beauty station and they started talking hair. Deb brought out pictures she had found in her wish box. She showed him variations on a bob-type style, ranging from modern and offbeat to old-fashioned and retro.

A Haircut Supreme was an odd slice of ordinary business left intact, a spot where the tornado of crisis did not touch.

"I sort of like my hair the way it is," she told him, "but I also don't like it."

He wasn't going to mention coloring; it was never wise to mention coloring with a new client who was just starting to turn gray.

"What don't you like about it?" he asked.

"It gets in my way, it's always blowing in my face, long hairs fall out and stick to my sweaters. I think it looks unkempt. I want something that looks neater, simpler."

Perhaps even more professional, she was thinking, considering where she had to go and what she had to do.

"How much styling do you do in the morning?"

"Oh, none, I never do that! I need something that's wash and go."

He looked at the photographs and then at her. He pointed to the modern one. The woman was blond, her hair chin-length, somewhat straight and curving this way and that.

"I think this is the one for you. It's the most natural. See how the others are poufed up in the back? You have to style to get that. I'd do this haircut a little differently to suit your face and hair type. What do you think?"

"Sounds great to me. I hardly ever get an official haircut."

"What made you decide to come in?"

She thought it had just been a whim, a comfort as she confronted her aging image, but suddenly she realized it was more than that: she had a mission, and the haircut was part of getting closer to her story. She was going to have to backtrack a little to find the little splinter and tell the story of its pain.

She decided as she spoke, "I have an event coming up, and I thought I'd use it as an excuse to get a haircut."

"You never need an excuse for pampering. What kind of event is it?"

Silly word, pampering, but she appreciated his interest in the event.

"I'm going to Story Pool," she told him.

Story Pool was the place where actors tested ideas for *The Story Pool Reporter* magazine, which covered participation in stories that had passed the actors' test of being chosen for discovery. Any story chosen to be acted out could then be reenacted. Participation in reenactments was the currency of stories.

"Story Pool? Does that still exist?"

It was in Canada now. A few actors were still involved. Joe had sent her an ad Ruth had placed in *The Story Pool Reporter* years ago without his knowledge: *Wanted, someone to find or create a teaching story about how to avert a crisis foretold.* Something that could happen ten or twenty years later, like the idea of suicide sneaking up on a healthy elderly person who would prefer to die with grace in due time, rather than in a compulsion of self-destruction.

She took the yellowed ad out of her pocket and handed it to Shawn.

"Read this. Do you know anything about this story?" she asked.

Deb had called her former contacts at Story Pool and learned that no one had ever answered the ad. The plea still haunted Deb; it seemed to point to something she must find before she was old, if she was going to get old.

"No, there is no such story. That's not how it goes, sorry. I mean, if the crisis were averted, we wouldn't be where we are today. Feel how soft your hair is. I'm just putting a little gel on to style it, but it's going to want to curl under by itself, the way I'm cutting it. You don't have to do all this; this cut will wash and go. I'm just fussing over it because I want you to look fabulous at your event. Were you invited?"

"Not necessary, I still have my media locket."

It made a series of soft gong sounds when she opened it. That still worked to gain the silence of entry.

"Are you dumping a story into the pool?" he asked.

Story Pool had a theater space that was in a pool so that viewers would see everything from above, a God's-eye view. Contributing was often called "dumping," which was not considered derogatory, just a natural process, like pilgrimage was for salmon. Even though there were no salmon left, their legend was still passed around.

"Think I do have something to dump," she said.

Deb thought about how different words had come into use. She used to hear the word "wrangling" on the news all the time: world leaders wrangled over this and that, and Congress wrangled over the budget. She was old-fashioned to think in terms of struggle this way rather than simply grieving. This was what the word "dump" was all about, just letting, letting the tears, the piss, and the shit come. She still struggled; she still believed in struggle, and in power struggles. There was a Bible story Jim/dad told her about Jacob, who meets an angel in his dream and wrestles it to the ground. The angel nearly kills him, but then the man finds that he has been touched by God, and he is blessed all of his days. So Deb thought there was something to be gained in struggle. *Wrestle your angel until you win angelic light.*

"Your hair is the perfect weight, not too heavy, not too light," Shawn was saying, hypnotically placing the affirmation in her subconscious: perfect weight, not too heavy, not too light. "Everything about it is perfect for the haircut I'm giving you. What do you think?" He gave her a mirror so she could see the back of her haircut as well as the front.

"I like it. I like the line you've created. It looks almost sleek," Deb said.

"Well, thank you for being open to trying something new and giving me the opportunity to create an excellent haircut today. Now I need to be quiet and concentrate on making sure it's just right."

Deb noticed the scene all around her, other stylists chatting it up with their clients, but the words became a sea of abstract sound. The hum of the blow-dryer and the even strokes of the comb through her hair mesmerized her. She looked out large windows facing the waterfront and thought about her encounter with the crystal ball: what it had said and how it said it so sternly, almost scolding.

She was simply being asked to do what she was good at doing, though she hardly believed she was good at anything anymore. She had been independent and successful even as a teenage single mom. She had become a professor. She once had fans and a career as a combination playwright and travel writer—a reality writer, they called her, the highest compliment, she thought. Now she spent most of her time doing chores. Charles had basically rescued her after her career fizzled; her voice and her vision seemed to have lost their place and power.

Now she was being asked to come up with something! Ha. Where did this demand come from? Her solar plexus? Her guts? What if she hid it squirming in her spleen, loitering in her liver, lolling in her gall bladder, fluttering undigested somewhere in her system? What then? Would she fall ill and die? Ha! Her life was hard work, what she and Charles had to do to survive. When it was warm, there were beekeeping chores and the tasks involved in building their house, as well as general homesteading activities. They lived without electricity or running water, and when it was too cold or too hot, the chores weren't pleasant.

How could she write a book now? At first she'd just wanted the story, but now the image of a book came to her. She imagined herself holding it, how it felt to know everything inside it by heart. A book was a body. A story without a book was just an idea. Like Shawn said, it was somehow less real, like scissors snipping the air. While Shawn checked and snipped every last bit of unevenness in her hair, a desire grew in her to make the image she was getting become a reality: her book, the story of A Crisis Averted in print. She was worried about how to tell Charles, now that she had decided she was going to write a book. Could one be true to oneself without being a slouch of a spouse? Part of her had never gotten used to being a spouse.

On the way back home, she stopped at an Internet kiosk and started searching for a portable word processor, apparently a forgotten technology. It was slow going; the computer was ancient and ill maintained. Now and then the electricity blinked off, and she would have to start over. Electricity was scarce at the edge of town; the heart of town often borrowed what it needed, being in an energy-priority zone.

Middleburg had always been a small town, a college town, and this type of communal center was perfect for the transition into the self-sufficiency of these times.

Deb discovered an Alpha Smart still available for the "Education Industry." She played her old professor card and posted "swap" for it on EdThing. She won her item at midnight and stayed there until

1:00 a.m., when it was delivered to her at the kiosk.

After the encounter with the crystal ball, Deb started writing in the mornings, putting in a few hours each day. She had imagined that she would go out and get the story, capture it, translate it, or find it in the rubble of a lost civilization. She used to think the story was deliberately trying to escape her, or that she might have to resort to choking it out. She imagined enemies hiding in the bushes, trying to get the story first. Now, she was not some kind of rodeo queen. She had the sense that the story was seeking her, trying to show itself and be understood.

Vocation was at the center of Jim's crisis. He hated the people of the church in Texas where he was doing his internship. He was hostile toward his mentor. After work, instead of bursting through the door and saying, "Hi honey, I'm home!" he sat outside in the car, refusing to come inside for hours. Grace found a note he had written, saying, "I want my mother." And on the advice of the wife of the supervising minister, she sent him home to his parents in Mobile, Alabama, where she expected his father would line up some psychological help. But neither his father nor his mother ever sent him to a psychiatrist. After a while, his father called and said, "He misses his family," and sent him back.

A rather unclean break from the ministry left Jim with a residue of failure.

He went on to take less challenging jobs to recuperate from his seminary fiasco. He hadn't jumped out of a window at this point in his story, but a deep depression was brewing. The target of his animosity had been his mentor, the supervising minister. Only when that target was out of view did he turn on himself. He had been depressed for months, maybe even years before the crisis fully wrought itself upon him. He endured severe psychosomatic symptoms like athlete's foot. As a bus dispatcher for Greyhound, he felt like he was too good, and at the same time not good enough. *Supposedly the spiritual purpose of having a job is to mitigate egoism.*

Deb always imagined that her granddad's sense of failure was due to lack of enthusiastic response to his sermons. She imagined that he had a boring voice and timid ideas. It was all about performance in her mind. Jim wanted to be a preacher, but Deb imagined that he hadn't counted on the reality of performance and tough crowds. He must have hated his mentor, the supervising minister, because of the contrasting glory raised by the other man's word-performance.

In fact, Jim's sermons were praised. It was only his attitude that was bad.

Jim had calluses on his vocal cords from using his voice the wrong way as a schoolteacher. Before he began to speak, he paused, making small preliminary sounds. It was easy for Deb to imagine that he failed at the charisma part of preaching. Yet charisma wasn't really expected of Presbyterian preachers, and being boring wouldn't have been considered a failure. To Deb, he seemed like a comedian who got booed off the stage and never came back. She didn't know what Jim/dad was like before she was born, before the calluses formed on his vocal cords.

After Jim failed, he tried to find another way to accomplish things. After he succeeded, he would try to succeed at things he had failed at before. For instance, he tried to learn jokes and retell them; this was like a failed sermon reincarnated as a successful punch line. He learned to start with something easy, like working at Pic-a-Pack as a clerk. There, he was a regular clean-shaven workingman, wearing a proud name patch. He had to be able to do that before he could become a teacher—the occupation that saved his life. Teaching was a hard job; he knew it was, and the fact that he had become a teacher was some sort of salvage of his life, a meaningful way to serve. But he was unaware of his strategy, so he had no faith in himself at all. He was miserable.

Not everyone got suicidal as they approached their dreams, even if those dreams seemed diminished in real life. Some people stuck to their ideals, even though the world was not encouraging.

Some found encouragement from a few friends and found that to be enough. After the accident, Grace and Jim had each other. His misery was mitigated by Grace but not completely absolved because he still did not know that he had a valid way of processing success and failure. He didn't see himself as in charge of his process. The creator is in charge, Jim thought. He was wishy-washy, never sure of anything. He went from being unbearably miserable to bearably miserable. Deb surmised some of this from what Jim had told her.

After Charles returned, Deb found it very difficult but not entirely impossible to continue writing. She hoped to find A Crisis Averted by writing down every layer of compassionate hindsight over Jim's story, and anything else that could possibly be a clue to the transformative narrative she was seeking.

Charles came home with a different enthusiasm. They worked on the land the next day because the weather was good, and there were no pressing beekeeping tasks at the moment.

They rolled gigantic logs over the rocky lumps of their land and into log stacks to dry for future building. They had many logs stacked and dried from prior years, but had not managed to mortar up more than a practice cordwood wall that held back the garden where Deb liked to sit, looking out to the west to see the sunset through the trees.

"There's something black and furry flying around my head," Deb said.

"I see it. That must be part of this dark cloud you've had around your head all morning. Remember our song . . . 'Always look on the bright side of life!' " He began to whistle it.

"This is a nice round log," she said, and Charles put his hand up for a high five. They bent over, one, two, three, and started rolling the log over a lump together. It was the lumpy ground Deb was resenting. Why couldn't it be smooth and easy to navigate without twisting an ankle? She never had twisted her ankle, but that seemed like a miracle.

Charles never made her feel bad about being a slacker, a weakling, or an evasive and whimsical person, when it came to building a house or keeping bees. He always seemed to accommodate her style as much as possible when they tried to get things done together. Charles was a hard worker, but he wasn't a martyr. He actually appreciated the difference in their attitudes and abilities. Deb was a thinker. She liked being active but not to the point of suffering. She liked being the idea person. Sometimes she came up with ideas just so they could take a break from the physical work and talk about them.

"Charles, let's try moving this one end over end, lift one end and let it flop over. Then let's take a break and decide which method works best."

"I can see where this is going," he said, but he

went along with her idea. He was thirsty.

They had talked briefly the night he got home about her birthday and how she had used the karma card. He seemed distracted and unimpressed with Deb's Alpha Smart, much less her haircut. But it was late at night and he was tired, so she tried not to hold it against him. In the morning, as usual, he was ready to go with an action plan for the day, including Deb as helper.

It was easier to dump the logs end over end to get them near the stacking area, except when the log was too fat to lift. As long as they were sitting and talking and having a drink, Deb had something else on her mind.

"From now on, I'm going to write for five hours every morning," she told him.

"Every morning? Five hours? How will we ever get anything done?"

"I'll wake up early, stay in my pajamas, and work for five hours, at least three. That's the only way I'll get this story done. Think about it. There are still other hours in the day for chores."

She didn't add that the spirit voice had said she had to write this book or she might get sick and die, but she was thinking of this authoritative backing of her plan. She could add that later, if need be. For now, he seemed to accept her authority and that was as it should be.

"I'm going to need you those other hours, but you go ahead and do what you have to do. I understand," Charles said.

One person had the right to designate a particular day as one's birthday, and that was the mother of that person.

"Deb, Debbie webby, Debbie cakes?" Charles called.

"What do you want?" Deb asked.

"Are you OK?"

"Yeah, why?"

"That noise you made, what was that?" Charles asked.

"Just a blip, a plippy whip," Deb said.

"Plippy whip, eh?" Charles said.

"That's what I want for my birthday dessert!"

"Your mom called."

Her mother, Helen, had been dead for as long as Deb had been alive, but that didn't stop her from getting a call in for Deb's birthday. Helen had quite a voice when she was alive. Now she came back in the form of a screech owl once a year to deliver a birthday gift to Deb. Helen could give her anything as long as it was free. All gifts from the spirit world had to be free. How did Deb miss her call? Was that the plippy whip noise she blipped, her mother's screech owl voice?

"Did you hear me? Your mom called!"

"Why?" Deb asked, wanting him to say it.

"For your birthday, you plippy whip! She wanted to remind you of her gift, and not to be late."

Deb's mother gave her high school enrollment for her birthday. Deb was a PhD, but she had missed part of high school. It had something to do with satisfying Helen's idea of thriftiness, Deb thought. High school education was free, and everyone should get one whether they had a PhD or not.

Somehow, Deb was not embarrassed to attend high school, even at her age. She accepted the gift as a challenge. She was used to accommodating her mother. Receiving these gifts was the only gift she could give to her mother. It was their relationship. Grandma Grace had tried to fill the role of mother. The only thing was, Deb knew she wasn't her real mother. She wasn't the one who really knew who she was and what she needed spiritually. Deb learned to mother herself early on. Grace had never intended to be a mom; her son, Dezy, had been an accident. When Deb pressed for details about childbirth, Grace replied simply, "It was excruciating."

The first day of school was today, Deb's birthday apparently, and she was five minutes late. Being on time was a big deal in high school, she realized, as she looked for a good spot to park her bike. All the racks were taken or reserved. She circled in confusion, not sure which door to go in. Then she heard over the loudspeaker, "If today is your birthday, you will be excused for being late. Be sure to tell office personnel if it is your birthday and you are late."

Deb went to the office and they got out her enrollment paperwork. Summer school had just started up, and the office was full of special cases, mostly punky young girls and sullen boys. The kind of kids Deb would have been afraid of when she was that age. As a young girl, Deb was shy, afraid of loud noises, and painfully unconventional.

The principal said, "I see here that you have a baby?"

Deb proudly confirmed, "Yes, I do, and she is all grown-up now."

That was the last documented comment they had on file for her. Amazing how pieces of the system persisted as if it were only yesterday she had been sixteen. It reminded her of a Chinese saying: Even the most faded ink outlives memory. The things recorded in ledgers still existed. Pregnant in high school! Ha, such a remote possibility now, though it would still be frowned upon if it did happen. Fertility rates were down across the board due to food, water, and genetic contamination, not to mention the damage laptops and cell phones did before they fell into disuse. The lifestyle of humans for the last fifty years had taken its toll, but responsibility was more in style than ever.

People started looking at her, and at each other for reactions. Deb wasn't sure if it was because of her age or because the principal had just announced she had been a teenage mom. Time shrank in that moment, bringing her into a slightly unpleasant peer relationship with the kids in the room, making her food for gossip, legend, and social politics. Pretty girls whispered to each other; boys stuck out their feet. A heavyset girl with an Afro slapped her on the back. Deb leaped up and screamed. The girls laughed and the boys cleared the room. The principal, a bald man wearing glasses and a collared shirt woven with the pattern of red graph paper, took a deep breath and sighed as he handed Deb her class schedule.

As she was about to leave, she remembered how academics could be mines of technical details. She turned around and said, "Today is my birthday."

"I know," he said. "We got that. Your mother called."

The secretary took a flower from the vase at the front desk and handed it to her. "Happy birthday!" she said.

Deb smiled and took the flower, a tiny yellow rose with red-edged petals. She took out a hankie to wrap the thorny stem. Just outside the office, she dampened the hankie at a water fountain. She put the wad in a side pocket of her backpack, letting the flower head stick out.

The halls were empty and she was late. What kind of education could she get in high school now? What had her mother wanted for her?

∽ CHAPTER 6 ∽

Deb didn't finish high school the first time around because she was pregnant with Miranda. She and the boy were both young and inexperienced when unexpected circumstances threw them together one evening.

She never thought of herself as an ordinary girl, the kind who falls in love or gets pregnant. As a child she preferred stuffed animals to dolls. Jim/dad called her Danny when he wanted her help with some manly home-chore. She never minded; these tasks seemed better than mopping the floor. She did think it was strange that he changed her name when they did certain things together, like building the garage. Motherhood was not in her plan, not ever.

Grace didn't recommend motherhood, and besides, Deb thought she would be too busy to have children. Busy doing what, she wasn't sure. She liked to read and to take pictures. She liked going on long walks and doing nothing. She didn't believe that she could get pregnant. The idea wasn't in her heart. Denial diverts radical action to fateful accident. She tried to make up for it all her life. She tried to be a good mother in her own way, after the fact.

Miranda did not announce her presence when she first took form in utero. Charles had a crush on Deb since grade school, but Deb, never a boy-crazy type of girl, remained asexual in attitude. Their relationship stayed preadolescent. They saw each other only at school and church youth group activities.

One of these activities was a white-water rafting adventure led by Deb's Jim/dad, along the Fifteen Point River. Jim/Dad was famous with the kids for his very scary ghost story. The story was simple, and he told it as if it were just a strange incident that happened to him one day. He told it only around the campfire as a last request. The story was this: On his way home from work teaching at an elementary school, he saw himself driving in the other direction in an identical car, in the other lane. The kids would ask him questions and he'd respond, raising the eerie factor with his excellent testimony of the incident. You could see he still felt the mystery of it, so it must have happened. No one could prove it didn't.

The kids found a whirlpool. They would jump in one end, and the water would take them under and spit them out in the same place every time, a little way downstream. It seemed pretty predictable and this tempered anything scary about it. Jim was totally OK with everyone jumping into the whirlpool—one at a time, of course. Deb was afraid to go in, and only after much encouragement did she hold her nose and take the plunge.

The moment when Deb should have popped up in the popping-up place, she didn't. Charles jumped in after her, even though officially that was against the rules; it counted as two at a time.

It would soon be dark, and Jim was not about to start a search party with a bunch of fifteen- and sixteen-year-olds at night. After a frantic flashlight search of nearby shores, he insisted that everyone go to their tents and go to bed, lights out and no talking. Of course there was whispering, but Jim could not tolerate anything more out of control than that. Though he had mellowed since his schoolteacher days, he was still prone to turning red and speaking harshly if things got out of hand. Neither he nor the kids were too worried about Deb and Charles. Deb was a Goody Two-shoes, and Charles was the son of a merchant marine and seemed to know everything about survival in water and on land.

Whirlpools passed Deb like a baton in a relay race. Charles followed until they were tossed to shore without their swimsuits. They were tired and it was cold. The night was long and they stayed close, struggling to keep each other warm. Early in the morning, they started back along the shore the way they came. They soon stumbled upon some abandoned clothes and put them on. No explanation was needed for the clothes upon their return. Who wanted to sleep in a bathing suit? Everyone was just happy that the incident had resolved itself and that everyone was safe. The feeling was one of euphoric relief. Deb was known as a scaredy-cat and a quiet girl, so it didn't occur to anyone that she would do anything wrong. Charles was a boisterous boy, but too immature to be seriously interested in girls—they thought.

That was the only night it could have happened. It took Charles and Deb a long time to figure out that she was pregnant because the pregnancy tests kept coming out negative. Charles was really interested in this, while Deb was completely aloof, sure she wasn't pregnant and uninterested in the possibility. She knew she was not the motherly type and would never have a child. Never. Charles was fascinated with feminine creativity and all the danger that it implied. Month after month, he insisted they check. Deb knew the facts of reproduction better than most kids her age because one of her favorite authors, May Sherwin, wrote about men, women, and their sexual biology. Still, she seemed in denial about her potential as a woman. Charles didn't know exactly how it worked; he was just convinced that it was the beginning of something new.

Charles had liked Deb since third grade when he taught her how to make a helicopter with her ruler, spinning it on a pencil and letting it fly. He admired the projects she brought in for show-and-tell: dozens of hand-sewn creations, a variety of red purses with buttons and stuffed kittens made from a sweatshirt. The year Deb got very sick was one lonely year for Charles. When she came back from the hospital the next year for fourth grade, he vowed he would never let her die "on his watch," a phrase he got from his father.

Miranda was about the size of a grapefruit in Deb's belly, still an unnoticeable change in her appearance, when the tests showed positive results for pregnancy. They had learned in their civics class that they had the right to remain silent, just as Miranda had been silent by not announcing her presence sooner.

Deb was an independent thinker and rather possessive about her daughter. She didn't turn to her parents, or to Charles. She ran away with her baby and lived like a wild woman. Deb was beautiful, though she did not know it, and this surely helped her get through all her adventures— alone, but never for long. *I may not always make my own money, but I make up my own mind, she thought*. All Charles got were letters and later visits with Miranda.

Though she was never deeply depressed by the difficulties of being a single teenage mother, she saw that like Jim/dad, she had the seed of suicide within her. It developed slowly, she imagined, on a distant to-do list, the ultimate exit plan. At times, she felt overwhelmed, felt crappy about her whole hopeless story. But Miranda always seemed happy, and that gave Deb a different focus.

Miranda married a daredevil. *Her husband, Ramey, was addicted to thrills.* She was traveling when she first met him in Cairo. He was working at a new American-themed park, stringing up lights on the Dip of Death. They had a cat named Raison. Ramey extended Deb's family now, like a son, even though she had never met him in person. *I have a good feeling about Ramey. Even though his plans for a bicycle trip into the Grand Canyon, now across the Mississippi Sea, fill me with worry, and even though he keeps Miranda so far away from me with these adventures, just knowing that Ramey loves Miranda, will take care of her, and be her family is enough to make me love him too.*

Every scrap of life in these times, you had to hang onto and love, because that was all there was to give you hope and joy, so she added the cat and Ramey to the treasures of her heart. The loss of life on this planet had happened slowly and then it had happened faster. Children inherited stuffed toy versions of animals that no longer existed: dolphins, gorillas, panda bears, leopards, and even plain old ducks. *Just focusing on taking care of someone near and dear, loving and being kind where you could, seemed the only thing anyone could do to counter the grief of our doomed world.*

Deb puzzled over a present for Miranda's birthday, hoping to celebrate it when she returned. Thirtysomething Miranda had only found Ramey last year. She had to go all the way to Cairo to find someone she wasn't related to. Such were the dangers of small populations. A present representing both homeyness and adventure would be perfect. Miranda liked riding her bike. Strength and independence were part of her style. Perhaps something bicycle powered for the home. She was a great cook too. As a child, she and Deb had enjoyed cooking together. Combining the two, Deb came up with: a bicycle-powered blender! Human-powered machines were in vogue now, the kind of antiques you might have seen years ago at the Tunbridge World Fair, such as a pedal-powered sewing machine or a treadmill-powered potato washer. Modern machines were retrofitted to run on human power, such as the pedal-powered washing machine.

CHAPTER 7

"How was school today, little Debbie?" Charles teased.

"There was a bomb threat," Deb lied as if she were fifteen again. "Did you make me an after-school snack?"

"How about some bread with honey and a glass of tea?" Charles humored her.

"Sure," she said and plopped on the couch. "Don't you want to hear about the bomb threat?"

"Yeah, I'll be right over. Let me slice the bread."

"Well, it was right in the middle of gym class, and we were all naked, and nobody could find their clothes except me because my clothes were all one-of-a-kind Lecturing Ladies originals. So I jumped into my clothes and ran out the door. Then I felt bad about all those young girls arguing over whose shorts were whose, about to be blown up, so I got on the loudspeaker and announced that today was Birthday Suit Day, and everybody came out, and I saved the day."

Charles came over and sat with her. "You're such a savior. You saved my day, too."

"Which one?"

"I can't remember. There have been so many. But each one counts, you know. They're all knitted together—if one of them is lost, none of the ones after turn out right."

"Have they been turning out right?"

"Perfect. Tea and toast," he said, gesturing toward the tankard of hot water, tea-making supplies, and a cutting board with bread. They said "toast" when it was only bread. Toast was a nice idea but too much trouble without a toaster.

"That wasn't true about the bomb threat, but we have to write a paper." She made a face.

"What are you going to write about?"

"I'm going to write about the issues of our times."

"Whoa . . . don't you think 'What I did on my summer vacation' would be more on target?"

"I'll call it one-third of the bottom half and throw in some bigger issues."

Deb believed stories could help people. She convinced her dear friend, clinically depressed Norm, that there was some beneficent force out there that warranted faith, and after death your spirit continued on. He was a complete unbeliever. She believed in eternity and reincarnation. All life circulated back into the web of life and the world of eternity in her view.

For years she sang, "What is the ultimate truth?" to the tune of an old hymn, and her answer came into being. She pried herself out of a paralyzing fear that gripped her in the night and dared to ask, "What is God?" and a light came into her darkness. Deb found her beliefs this way, by asking questions, and the answers imagination provided were real. She didn't know exactly what God was, but she saw a need in Norm, and her stories illuminated something to that order. She had a way of teaching subjects she didn't know much about by drawing on collective bits and pieces of knowing.

Deb was not a people person, so she tended to see God as a light or a force rather than a being. The key was the need to know, and at the same time an acceptance of uncertainty.

When Norm denied spiritual reality, his mother got upset. It was a difference between them over something they shared: the loss of his brother, her son. Norm's mom didn't have religion, but that was no excuse for atheism. Everything happened for a reason. She kept her concerns to small everyday matters, and left the big things up to God.

"We are all made of particles. Energy never dies but is only transformed so that the particles fall apart and come together in new ways. Even if we are only compost, from our lives and from our bodies come new lives and bodies. Does it matter if we remember the process?" she told him as she imagined spontaneously. "I remember being in spirit, or nothingness. And from this nothingness, I found my star, a place I remembered, and I came to this planet to continue my transformation of energy. Did you know that there is only a tendency for particles to be here or there? Nothing is certain." She threw in some scientific information that appealed to her. "Perhaps we flicker in and out, but permanent spirit death seems unlikely. More likely, we are reincarnated. The spirit likes to wander and experience things from different points of view."

Making up a story, Deb recounted her life as a pear tree; she had flowered and then artfully spattered to the ground her pale pink petals. The squirrels used to tickle her arms as they played in her branches and tasted her fruit. Then she told of her life as a bird. She whistled a high trilling melody— Deb was a good whistler—she had taught flowers to bloom with this song. Lastly, she told about her life as a gorilla, how quiet and serene it had been, the security of her primate family, the daily grooming and politeness. A gorilla knew how to enjoy both solitude and familial warmth, she said. The gentle vegetarian gets plenty of space to quietly be. And of course, you could spend eons in space without ever incarnating. The creative spirit is yours forever to use as you wish. These last ideas appealed to Norm: he liked imagining himself as a high-status silverback gorilla, or if not that, then yes, spending eons in the sky without ever incarnating.

Norm could see Deb's thoughts in pictures. After a while of seeing the eternal natural kindness of the universe in which we continually transform, he just said, "OK, I believe you." After that, he started studying Hinduism. He feared his special goddess, Kali, because she wore men's arms as a fringe for her skirt. He prayed that he would not reincarnate, which was perfectly appropriate in Hinduism. He continued his study, and considered himself a student of Hinduism rather than a believer. *That is every bit as good if not better than being a believer.* Her story helped him. She was proud of that.

Deb asked Buddha to be her guide when she went to Story Pool. *Why not? He's the guy, right? It's good to have a spiritual guide when you go to Story Pool.* She had heard stories about Buddha sitting under a tree, and had seen statues of him in museums looking cool, relaxed, and peaceful. No way was she going to ask Jesus to be her guide; too much sadness and suffering, being hung upon the cross and all, blood dripping from the nails in his hands. She wouldn't ask Mary either, as she was part of the same punishing story. Siddhartha, he went looking for what he wanted and became Buddha, so yeah, she was going to be like that, shoot straight to the heart and win serenity. Sometimes you just had to make a choice. Buddha could mean a lot of different enlightened beings anyway; it was a very popular name. Buddha this, Buddha that. *Other names are so hard to remember. Other faces are not so universal.* Buddha could just be a rock, sitting so still. He might be in that rock by that tree.

Story Pool was a shadow of its former self. The pool floor was no longer blue green; hardly a chip of the old paint remained. The stadium-quality bleachers had been replaced with rustic benches reminiscent of a summer camp. The theater was outdoors. Even when it was in Vermont, it had been outdoors, but the lobby had always been like the lobby of a fancy old inn. This part was severely degraded, and now resembled the lobby of a social service organization. A plump, attractive woman in her fifties staffed the front desk. Chin-length locks of almond-brown sliver-streaked hair framed her face, curling slightly forward like friendly vines. Deb was glad to see a welcoming face, and surprised that she recognized the woman as the one who had always been at the front desk of Story Pool.

"Marlene?"

"I'm surprised you remember me. I've put on so much weight, but you look exactly the same, except your hair is a little saner."

"You look great, Marlene. How did you manage to put on weight?"

"It's job related. I found out that it wasn't just a saying, 'starving artists.' These actors were really starving. And I just had to do something. These actors do so much for us out of their passion to present the truth, and we nearly went under because the actors were dying of starvation—I don't know how we missed the signs, but before you knew it, literally skeleton crew."

"How did you turn it around?"

"I reenvisioned this place as a social service organization. You'd be surprised how much people will give once you educate them."

"You're a genius!"

"I can't stand to see anything go to waste," she said, patting her belly and nodding.

She nodded so emphatically, Deb found herself nodding in agreement. Then she noticed a candy dish of Pips.

"Help yourself," Marlene said.

"Don't mind if I do." Deb smiled and pocketed a few. "Do you still need to hear my media locket?"

"Don't worry about it. I'll tell you a secret: basically, nothing gets rejected anymore."

"You're kidding?"

"Nope. I see you have some papers, and I guarantee the actors will seize on them immediately."

It was said that only the actors at Story Pool decided if something was true or not. If the actors could not act it, then the story had no truth. She wanted to get her feet wet with story writing again. It had been a long time since she had done anything professional.

"If you'll just sign this waiver," Marlene said.

"What's the waiver for?"

"Truth or consequences."

"What?"

"You haven't been around in a while. Story Pool no longer validates stories, or in your case any other written material. But if you ask me, it never really did, only for people who believe in outside validation."

Deb signed the waiver and backed away, but not before a skinny bald man wearing shades rushed forth and grabbed the papers.

He sniffed the papers and started to twitch. He signaled to a woman with a sharp nose, and they looked at the papers and went down into the pool. The stage manager started getting things ready, moving things around. The play began:

The scene is set as a typical 1970s living room. The sharp-nosed woman attends to her husband, who has just arrived home amid suspicion. She picks up a thread trailing from his shoe, and asks, "Why were you searching for voodoo on Whobook?"

The man sits down in an armchair and lights a pipe.

"I was taking an apitherapy course, and one of the presenters was concerned about how we as apitherapists present ourselves. 'We don't want people to think of apitherapy as some kind of voodoo,' he said. I told him we don't know enough about voodoo to be speaking of it in a disparaging way. People from New Orleans or Haiti might be offended. In the catalogue of expired courses, voodoo is described as a religion. I thought it was a philosophy. I thought maybe there was a social network of legitimate voodooists on Whobook. Anyway, I believe in suspending judgment, and finding out more. That's why I was searching for voodoo on Whobook."

The woman has been lighting tea candles, which she arranges in a filigree pattern on the coffee table. "Why did that stranger give you his jacket?"

The man gets up from his chair and starts pacing and gesturing with his hands.

"He believes in freedom of expression, or more accurately, free expression, giveaway expression. Each thing, no matter how complicated, no matter when or from whence it sprang, is a letter of the alphabet. I was washing off an Egyptian pictograph of a lion in the sink when I realized this, blue ink escaping everywhere. All things are elements of language, tools of expression. No sooner has someone made something original than it becomes material for further expressions. It's a fractal sort of thing. A sacred DNA within the DNA. I heard on the radio recently that the whole idea of the spiral for DNA was stolen from a woman scientist, before there were woman scientists!"

"That was a very good answer," says the woman. "Now I am going to have to ask you the same question I have asked you before: Why have I not met your parents?"

He regresses and turns himself into a little boy. He puts on his slippers and looks into his hands. "Because I am an orphan. I lost my father when he fell into a rabbit hole. At first it was just his foot, then his leg. Eventually, the rabbit got a good hold on him and pulled him the rest of the way down. Rabbit holes look innocent, but a whole foot can fit inside, and if you aren't careful, your whole leg could slip in and then, well, people have been known to disappear."

". . . And your mother?" the woman asks.

"My mother fell in love with a lion. She could have killed him. She had a knife and she was ready. But when the lion got near, she wanted that strong warm sinewy fur near her, wanted his weight upon her. She told the lion, 'I am in love with you so do not eat me.' The lion played with his food and then ate her. He tore her soft body apart so that it was unrecognizable as human flesh. He ate her heart whole. Somehow, the lion connected her heart to his and lived as a two-hearted lion."

The woman makes room for him in the chair, and they share a sad hug as lights dim and the story ends. The filigree of tea candles glows.

As Deb left Story Pool, fistfuls of snow were coming down. The ground, which had been bare moments ago, was now covered. It was hard to see; her glasses were instantly coated. In the cloud of snow with her was a young woman. The wind was blowing and slapping them with generous gusts of snow. Deb turned around and walked backwards to fend off the slappings. The two remarked upon the weather in amazement. "I heard there was going to be a storm," the other woman said.

They could hardly see outside their cloud of snow. Normally, they probably wouldn't have said a word to each other, two strangers, but here they were alone in a feisty snow globe. "I'm glad I'm not riding my bike home in this," the young woman said. "I only wish I had a hat."

"How far do you have to go? You really do need a hat."

Deb felt guilty as the woman's blond eyebrows filled up with snow. With hair the color of whipped egg whites, she looked barer than if she had been a brunette. How could Deb not feel guilty when she came prepared to change according the weather, while the blond had only the clothes she happened to be wearing? Deb felt overabundant with hats. She had on a mad bomber, earflaps clipped under the chin. Besides that, her coat had a detachable hood that was not detached.

Perhaps the young woman sensed that Deb was about to offer her a hat.

"I'm going back to campus," the woman said, and crossed the street.

An act of generosity requires intimacy, and the

101

intimacy of the snow bubble was illusionary. It seemed silly not to assume oneness with all creation, but one still came across "big-city" attitudes, or socially elite attitudes. Deb herself was defensive of her personal borders, at times repelled by the idea of oneness.

It was not necessary to cross the street to get to campus.

It wasn't until the young woman had disappeared that Deb noticed the only thing inappropriate about her own apparel for this unexpected weather: her loose-fitting shoes were filled with snow. Red leather Mary Jane clogs; she thought for once these would be just right for the occasion. She had washed and polished them in an effort to look the part of a reputable Story Pool submitter, but the part had been changed. She could have worn any shoes, or none at all. Story Pool had gone from elite intellectual powerhouse to social service organization, and no longer discriminated on the basis of shoes.

At one time, when she had money to spend on shoes, this was how she imagined herself: at leisure, pretty, well taken care of, professional, and smart. The shoes were no longer practical. Her life required her to do hard labor on rough terrain. But the pretty red clogs were easy to slip into, and she wore them more often than was appropriate. She had a long walk home and would have done better with hiking boots. Nonetheless, being prepared was a habit she had learned from Charles. In her backpack, she had a pair of rubbers that Miranda made for her. She took these out, brushed her shoes off, and stretched the black inner tube over. Perfect. She looked well taken care of, if not at leisure.

CHAPTER 8

There were three other students in Deb's class, on the third floor. A thin woman with cream-colored hair flowing through the back of her baseball cap walked slowly around the perimeter of the room. She straightened the globe, although it would have been impossible to know whether the globe was straight. She wore black sweatpants with white stripes down the sides, and a pale yellow T-shirt. Her tennis shoes were white and clean. The long, thick, straight hair, streaming out the back of her baseball cap, made her look like a lackadaisical and underdeveloped teenager from the back. Her loose and easy posture seemed to support that. But her hair wasn't platinum blond. It was white. She had been the phys ed teacher for many years, and she still taught tai chi. She always walked three times around the perimeter of the room before starting class. Deb, Joe, Tim, and Stevie were all there, waiting.

Three: the universal sign for distress, or perhaps a lucky number.

"Joe, are you going to read your paper

today?" Joe was at the sink with a rag, still trying to get his son Stevie cleaned up and ready for class.

"Sorry, Ms. Mushwhiler, I haven't gotten to it yet, but I've been thinking about it. I thought I'd write about the day I planted petunias."

Joe was deep in concentration, holding Stevie's chin in his long-fingered, articulate hands, wiping every last remnant of breakfast from Stevie's round, inner-focused face. Five-year-old Stevie endured the toddler treatment, allowing himself to be the object of his father's cleaning.

"Stevie, do you have a paper for me?"

Stevie didn't answer her. On the class roster, it said "mute" next to his name. But Ms. Mushwhiler tried to get everyone to participate. "Life is a team sport," she would say. Stevie's lanky big brother spoke up for him.

"We all wrote regular papers at our house, but a wild boar came in the night and ate them. He ate mine first, so he must have liked it the best."

"What? You watched him eat your papers!" Ms. Mushwhiler exclaimed.

"Who can not watch a pig eat? He ate with such joy, we couldn't take our eyes off him. He shook his head to get Dad's papers out of the huge clip that held them together and would only eat two pages—the part about the petunias."

Ms. Mushwhiler didn't want to debate the issue of wild boars. A pig, imagined or real, would steal the show before you knew it, and this was her class, her show to run.

"Deb?" Ms. Mushwhiler prodded.

"Yup," said Deb, "I have it right here."

"Well, read it," Ms. Mushwhiler said, taking her clipboard and sitting at one of the students' desks.

Deb walked to the front of the class and proceeded to read her paper:

> Two-thirds of the bottom half and other issues of our times, by Deb Exlander

> I have distilled and transcribed a long telepathic exchange between myself and my daughter, Miranda, crystallizing it into a nine-point star to illuminate our times. I believe that what we have lost in speed, we have gained in direction. These nine issues point to how very slowly, almost imperceptibly, we are going in the right direction.

> I chose nine points because the qualities of the number nine, perfection, balance, and transition from death to rebirth, are the qualities by which we can understand our times, the years beyond the years. Though these may seem to be the shabbiest and most regressive of times, never has humanity been on a more productive path. Here are the nine light-

giving attributes:

1. New forms of communication are being developed.

As the Internet has become less useful, and gradually retrofitted to our diminishing electronic capabilities, extra-personal abilities have emerged. While at present certain people, mostly women and children, are able to extend primitive technologies into psychic communication tools, this skill seems to be spreading according to use among the general population. Using only stones, herbs, and water, travelers can stay in touch with loved ones at home. People adept at using intention, faith, and associative thinking can send and receive pictures, words, and even virtual visits, all without "technology." This is very practical and also seems to be generating higher knowledge as has not been known since The Gita.

2. A few travelers are discovering new things about earth.

While fewer travelers are making their way around the globe than ever before, the travel experience has intensified and gained value. Travelers are exploring personal issues of trust and loyalty, staying with people, learning their customs and accepting hospitality. Travelers are challenged physically with sickness and emotionally with love. New places with unfamiliar streets or the act of eating strange food with new friends cause travelers to evolve at an accelerated pace. They return able to love across worlds, time, and space. They bring back discoveries about earth made though oneness consciousness. Sometimes called "the traveler's disease," oneness consciousness is the ability to hear and see the earth as it expresses itself.

3. People are building their own homes from the land, if able.

This oneness consciousness that travelers are bringing home has led to a new enthusiasm for families to build their own homes as a form of communication with the land. Plopping boxes on hills has lost its status. Now people talk to the land, dream with the land, and mutually grow a form that is livable inside and out, a place that meets their needs and celebrates the natural gifts of the place.

4. Addiction and recovery are the main models we have.

Addiction has been a big problem in recent decades. Two things have helped secure the gains that recovering addicts have made. First, the multiple fractal omissions of sensory and cerebral inputs since 2012 have confused the drug map in the synapses of recovering addicts to the point where relapse is not as accessible as it once was. Second, the age-old Twelve Steps still work as do many of the sayings, like accept what you cannot change. The recovered addicts in our society bring many gifts, with great difficulty, every day. They know themselves, and are tolerant of others. Those two big things have almost put an end to war. True, the economy has suffered, but it wasn't worth much even yesterday.

5. Travelers uproot natives to future trip and fall in love.

This is just a mysterious wonder, but almost no traveler who starts out alone comes home alone. Things seem so bad everywhere that there is no one who would not leave to be close to someone they have come to care about. Future tripping is beyond love; it is the ability to commit even with doubts about the outcome.

6. Animals are leading the way to sanity.

Though there are fewer animals and many species have perished, humans have finally learned to value them. Perhaps we only value what is scarce. The intense heat of recent years combined with random snow days and surprise rainy seasons has been hard on humans and animals. It is as if we are at sea with a couple of kittens, and we love them so because we are so lonely on this planet. Owls are once again giving advice in the forest, where people seek their wisdom. Nature is a treasured fairyland, a universal childhood, and any remaining scrap of that blanket is greeted with great glee.

7. Health and sickness are the main topics of intelligent conversation.

All the improvements to life that came to save the day when industry collapsed can be linked to faith and folk remedies. Discussion of health and happiness or sickness and down-spiritedness has strengthened the minds of the general public. With every way that people find to be well, a new faculty is learned and replaces old technologies that don't work anymore. Herbs, yoga, meditation, affirmations, Reiki, shamanism, apitherapy, and voodoo have replaced other unavailable means. Empowering manifestations have become necessary, and by talking openly about health and sickness, good possibilities are likely.

8. YesterDollars and karma cards make trivialities visible, and politics are avoided since we are all visitors anyway.

The purpose of YesterDollars and karma cards is to add old-fashioned details, a sort of decorative description to the passage of time. Spending is meant as a sort of accounting for experience: staying in huts, food, clothes, drinks, pharmacy stuff. Politics are only a protest against voting. The only real voice the people have is dance.

9. Distraction is our biggest problem, but it hasn't stopped the growing popularity of a long-sacred text, The Rita, a conversation between mother and daughter.

Distraction is the posttraumatic

stress of our times. We have been overwhelmed with problems, overwhelmed with impossibility, overwhelmed with desperate cries for attention, and now it is hard for anyone to concentrate. Most conversations drift off into a sense of . . . and what was I doing? Thinking? Talking about? Yet even with this huge scar from the disasters we have limped through, The Rita, the long conversation between mother and daughter, has accumulated listeners, contributors, and devotees. The Rita is our greatest sign of hope.

"Any questions? Comments?"

Ms. Mushwhiler's clipboard was full of star diagrams. Joe, Tim, and Stevie were in a family pile on the beanbag couch.

Tim raised his hand. "How were you able to whistle and read your report at the same time?"

"Nobody leaves this classroom till we find out who was whistling during Deb's report."

"Ms. Mushwhiler, can I go get us all some tea so we can discuss this properly?"

"Yes, you may, Deb, but make it snappy."

Joe had an idea. "Let's move all the chairs out of the way and make a big nine-pointed star on the floor. Then we can collage in each of the nine points with images that speak to the points."

"Excellent idea, Joe. I'm glad someone was

paying attention."

"I was paying attention. I even had a question," Tim said.

Stevie, the "baby," was whistling in his sleep.

"Tim, that's as good a confession as I ever heard. You now have detention to serve Saturday morning. Case closed."

Meanwhile, Deb was stopped in the hallway by a pack of sixteen-year-old girls outside Room 99. They just pounced on her like she was fresh meat and robbed her of an entire tea service. She noticed one of the girls was wearing a poetry T-shirt.

Deb asked, "You like poetry?"

The girl gushed, "I love it, it is like so cool, I mean finally people just saying stuff, stuff so beautiful and true."

"Your face looks just like the portrait on the cover of a poetry book I have in my locker. I'll trade it for the tea service. What do you say?" Deb asked.

"OK, you go get it. We'll be right here waiting."

Deb went back to class and purposely forgot about the whole thing.

"No tea?" asked Ms. Mushwhiler.

"The teapot was broken," Deb said.

"All right, Miss No Tea, you and whistling Tim here can come in Saturday morning and prepare the nine-pointed star for the class to use in the art/science exposition," Ms. Mushwhiler announced.

Tim shrugged, raised his hand for a high five. Deb lazily pushed back at his hand.

Joe woke up Stevie in anticipation of Ms. Mushwhiler's "Class dismissed!"

Deb knew she would be put in a special class, because of her PhD. Or PHad, as Ms. Mushwhiler liked to call it. She just didn't realize how special. She was still trying to figure it out. There was the multiage thing, the family group thing, but what else was odd about this class? Oh, she fit in. It was a class of misfits. Stevie was only five and didn't belong in high school. Joe was too old for high school. Only Tim was the right age for high school, yet he was not with his peers. Deb had never fit in with her peers either. Family had interfered. Perhaps subconsciously, she had wanted to become pregnant. Becoming a mother at an early age helped her escape the constraining conformity enforced by teenagers and allowed her to express her independence. Still, there was something sad and isolating about never having tasted the elixir of approval or the shared experiences of growing up.

CHAPTER 9

It hadn't gone so badly, reading her paper. No one had criticized it, or even competed with it. In a weird way, an aura of cooperation surrounded everything since her encounter with the crystal ball. Everywhere she went, it was as if she brought a calming enchanted garden with her; the space around her was transformed.

She found the magic words, "I hear and I obey," then entered a sensitive world where every being and thing she encountered repeated those words back to her. Really, it was just quiet listening, a heightened observation of her connectedness to the world around her. She found the words while browsing the historical society's herb garden. She was not sure where the words came from. Was it the bee, the flower, or the garden as a whole that said them? She only knew that hearing this phrase in the garden made her part of the conversation, and that she had entered a listening sanctuary.

To be in a listening sanctuary was to enter into a world of alert service among all beings. "I hear and I obey," she repeated. A small flame burst from a flower; a gaseous cloud flared in streamers up to the sky and then disappeared without smoke. Had this energy come from her throat? She felt a transfer, a leap across the air between them. Partly frightened and partly amazed: the observer had responsibilities to do what needed to be done. She would call the historical society and let them know there was a small flare-up in the garden.

"A gas plant," they told her when she called. "*Dictamnus albus* and *Dictamnus purpureus*. It doesn't usually flare unless you put a lighted match just above the flowers. Are you sure there was no spark or fire nearby?" Deb was sure. She wondered if the plant had taken and purified something from her, perhaps anger she was unaware of.

What a feeling it was to know she had a place to be heard in her listener's sanctuary. She might be walking, taking a nap, or just sitting when these thoughts came to her like a soft blue blanket tossed from the sky.

There had been a storm, and Charles scored some fallen cedar from a neighbor. He was there bucking it up.

"With this cedar, I think we have all the wood we'll need!" Charles said.

"It's beautiful wood, the way it's red in the middle, and smells good. Maybe it will keep moths away?"

She noticed a rainbow light reflecting off everything: the glacial erratics, the logs, and especially Charles. An envelope of protective, powerful light, indigo, rainbow-edged, surrounded him as he nudged the air around himself.

It's only as youth expires that we reflect on the gift of life, she remembered Jim/dad saying. Why did she worry about her power to end it all when she was nearing the end at a nice clip anyway?

As she carried branches, she listed the reasons, one per branch in a growing pile of limbs:

I know I could do something impulsive like that, something crazy. The house isn't built yet; the road to restfulness seems long. I've done it before. And what if Charles dies, why should I live? It would be too much work to do alone.

That's it, it's the being alone part. It's the overwhelming tone that work takes when there is no one to help, the senseless drudgery of it all. Deb didn't like to ask for help. With Charles, she didn't have to.

She couldn't know what it was like for Jim. She inherited his rashness, not his rationale. She believed the suicide impulse was like a platonic form passed down through the DNA. Though she might narrate her story differently, she did the same things. She reenacted his life as if it were the Stations of the Cross, precisely to show it didn't have to be that way. *It didn't have to be a sad story, did it?*

Deb had a lot of secrets. No matter how much she disclosed, no matter how much she wrapped up

117

the darker business of her life, more untold stories seemed to crop up. Buried parts of her story heaved to the surface in the same way that the ground adjusted itself in spring to thawing winds. She felt funny when she didn't tell Charles about these things. The main person in her life didn't know the truth about things that surrounded them, like the blender, for instance.

There was a story, a biography of the blender that they had been using as a lamp since they got married, and Charles didn't know it. Sometimes she told a part of it, like, "I bought this blender at an antique shop for twenty dollars." But that didn't truly illuminate the blender and all it implied. There were many things that had happened in the blender's life, secret injuries and repairs. Even a blender's life could have meaning.

She didn't tell him the part about how she couldn't afford anything nice at the time, and how needy she had felt. She felt the need to spiff up her life with the dignity she had dreamed of. She was married to another man back then, a rich but terribly frugal man. She didn't like to ask for money. But there was an antique store within walking distance of where they lived, and the fine things she dreamed of were from the old days when they made things to last. She walked to The Fourth Wish Antique Shop and described something that should be in the shop but wasn't in plain sight. That was her usual technique. Then the owner would scratch his head and try to be helpful.

"A thick glass jar on an enameled metal pedestal, Art Deco in style. Do you have something like that?" The man searched his memory and then poked into various boxes in the barn. When he found it, she asked the price and he said fifty dollars. She never paid the asking price for anything, and she did not buy anything off the floor—only things that caused him to dig into the deep memory of the dusty old barn out back.

She said she liked the blender, but she couldn't afford fifty dollars and didn't think it was worth that anyway, since it was dirty and old but not refurbished. She offered twenty dollars, and he called her the worst Yankee that ever came into his shop, and sold it for exactly that.

She took her treasure home, cleaned it up, and began making what was one of her favorite dishes back then, chocolate milk shakes. Miranda loved this treat as well, and Deb allowed her to operate the blender and make the shakes herself. Back then they still had electricity, and Miranda rigged up an extension cord and set up her smoothie operation on a card table outside. She successfully made a nice batch and divvied it up into glasses on the table. As she carried the glass jar part of the blender inside, it slipped out of her hands and landed on the stone steps, breaking hopelessly into pieces. Deb knew Miranda was as upset as she was about it, so as she picked up the shards, she said only, "It's a good thing you poured out the milk shakes first. We'll find a new pitcher for the blender." It was a beautiful glass pitcher shaped rather like a flower with four petals. Deb looked everywhere for a new one. Miranda did, too. But in the end, no regular store had one, and Deb tried the antique store again.

Amazingly, the owner was able to dig one up. It wasn't exactly right: the bottom didn't fit into the blender pedestal, but it had the right aesthetic. It matched the quality and style of the old blender. Perhaps not wanting to haggle with her again, he gave it to her for free. Or maybe he was being kind. Whatever the case, it was lucky for Deb. If you didn't have money, you needed luck. Deb's then husband, Kurt, machined a piece of hard black plastic to fit between the old pedestal and the new glass jar so that the pitcher fit securely and looked like it was part of the original unit. *Should one feel guilty, undeserving of a gift?* She felt secretive about her luck.

The lid that came with the new pitcher was missing the removable plastic knob in the middle, but Deb was able to salvage the knob from the old lid. Finally, the blender was back together again after being rescued from the brink of life, and quality had been preserved as well as contentment in the family. She felt proud of her resourcefulness.

The blender represented determination and the fact that despite appearances, things were often patched rather than matched. In fact, before she had thought to purchase a blender, Kurt said something odd that stuck with her, "You can put two things in a blender and push a button, but you can never get those two things to be back as they were before." Deb had thought it was kind of a spooky thing to say. She knew he was talking about the two of them, but she didn't see getting married as going into the blender. She never shared the story of the blender with Charles because she never talked about her past relationships with other men.

Charles was the key, outlined in rainbow light, if she would take it. He offered to help. What greater assistance can God give than a human partner in life?

Charles walked across the empty dried mud of the house site.

"Charles, stop right there for a minute."

He stopped.

"Put down the chain saw."

He put down the chain saw. She came closer, looked at him, at the space around him, trying out different angles. He imitated her, curiously tilting his head.

She explained, "I've been seeing a rainbow light around you, and I was just checking to see if it was really there. I think it might be my glasses."

"Just around me?" Charles asked.

"Well, I see it around other things, too, like that rock over there."

"Oh, I'm like a rock to you, then, just like a

rock or a log or anything?"

"I don't know. It seems to appear especially around you, but I'm not sure it's really there at all."

"Aw, I thought I was special," he said, and picked up the chain saw

CHAPTER 10

Suicide came into Jim's mind the minute he left Texas. As he was driving away, he thought to himself, *this whole painful thing will be over now.* He had confronted the pastor with his anger, and they instantly dismissed him and sent him away. It happened without any transition, it seemed to Jim.

A year later, training to be a middle manager for Greyhound, a corporate job in a corporate culture, he saw his whole damn life before him, and it did not look good. He tried to end it, but that janitor cleaning windows down below foiled the suicide. Then his body's natural healing powers and his wife's loving care cinched the deal with life. He was back in, like it or not.

With medication and psychiatric care, he was able to get a teaching job in St. Bernard Parish. He, Grace, and young Dezy moved to an apartment in St. Bernard Parish, where they found a new church, The Evermore Believing Presbyterian. There, they met the Buckleys, the kind of friends who changed lives. Rich Buckley became friends with Jim after an incident at church. The congregation was saying the Apostles' Creed:

> I believe in God, the Father almighty,
> Creator of heaven and earth.
> I believe in Jesus Christ, his only Son, our
> Lord,
> Who was conceived by the Holy Spirit,
> Born of the Virgin Mary . . .

At that point Jim threw his prayer book at the minister and shouted out, "I don't believe it!"

Rich went and picked up the prayer book and brought it back to Jim. Jim then took the scripture and began reading the next lines along with the rest of the congregation:

> Suffered under Pontius Pilate,
> Was crucified, dead, and buried:
> He descended into hell;
> The third day he rose again from the dead;
> He ascended into heaven,
> And sitteth on the right hand of God the
> Father Almighty;
> From thence he shall come to judge the
> quick and the dead.
> I believe in the Holy Ghost;
> The holy Catholic Church;
> The Communion of Saints;
> The Forgiveness of sins;
> The Resurrection of the body,
> And the Life everlasting.
> Amen.

That was where the story ended for Deb. That was all she had been told. Now that Jim had entered his half-life, it was difficult to get information out of him. Grace and Jim/dad had died some years ago, though Deb was not sure when or how it happened. She knew it was less than ten years ago because they both would materialize and then spiritualize into thin air; plus they had stopped aging. It was a bewildering boon to have an extra interlude between life and death.

Jim tended to dematerialize when she asked questions about his past, and she got the feeling that reminiscing about the past was not how he wanted to spend his half-life. He had new hobbies that he liked to attend to. He would spend some days alone sailing in his Sunfish, and other days in the town chatting it up with whomever he could find. He and Grace traveled separately. Grace preferred to travel in spirit to faraway places. They were no longer very attentive to Deb.

*Could Dezy still be alive somewhere? He would have been a little boy when Hurricane Betsy came. We were both raised by Jim/dad—though at diffe*rent *times. Maybe he would have a different perspective, something to add to Jim's story?*

Oh God, it's such a soap opera. I'm too old to indulge in emotional long-lost father melodrama!

The fact that her real father had abandoned her as an infant was so far in the past now, at midlife it was a drop in the bucket, a minor detail with no significant effect on her life. However, this little detail that she had ignored for so long was squirming to the surface like a hope, or a bad idea.

She remembered finding his overcoat in a closet when she was young, and feeling she was onto some mystery-solving relic. It never occurred to her to harbor bad feelings about the circumstances of her birth; that didn't come till later. From her child's point of view, Grace and Jim/dad were indulgent parents, her late mother still sent magical birthday presents, and her father—well, she had never known him, so she couldn't miss him. It wasn't until she had a child of her own at a young age that she began to question the excuse that her real father was "too young" to assume the role.

What she felt as an echo of abandonment, Dezy would have experienced full force as his parents were sucked into his father's crisis. Grace must have something to say about her son, some clue as to his whereabouts. Deb decided to track her down.

Since Grace was always traveling, Deb sought out Jim/dad. He could more easily find Grace since they were both in half-life. She walked out to the Swap Spot where Jim/dad liked to sit and talk with neighbors. He was sitting in an old rocker playing the harmonica as she approached. She waved. He put the harmonica in his shirt pocket and waved back.

"Hi Pop, I'm looking for Grace, you seen her?"

"Not too much lately. She travels, you know."

"Why don't you go with her?"

"I like it here, I don't need to see the entire planet like Grace does. Besides, we traveled together often enough when we were alive."

Deb traced the porch railing with her hand, pulling a tendril of vine loose. Its little brown feet took pieces of wood with it. This type of vine was not the ivy of her childhood, whose tiny strings of leaves and tendrils wrapped themselves around whatever structure they could find. Deb lay down on a bench, suddenly tired. The sun seemed to bake in Jim/dad's last words as she rested . . . "When we were alive" . . . She wished he hadn't said that because it seemed he was alive, and a half-life was still a life. But Jim/dad saw some sort of difference; somehow, he had "crossed over" before completely leaving this world. Jim was waiting for her to say something. He kept patting his knees and looking over at her, but Deb's eyes were closed and she was still enough to tempt the vine to move in and envelope her. Nervously, Jim/dad put a hand on her shoulder.

"Let's go out on the ocean, that's where you'll find Grace if she is around here."

"You're not tired?" Deb asked. "You feel up to it?"

"Sure, it's my favorite thing to do, and it'd be fun to go out with you."

Deb had never been in the Sunfish with Jim/

dad. She was generally a little afraid of large bodies of water.

"OK," she said, swinging her legs off the bench to sit up. She would have to trust Jim/dad's sailing and that wasn't easy for her to do, except that she herself knew nothing about sailing. It might be fun, and anyway, she had to do it to get closer to her story.

They walked around to the back of the Swap Spot, where the Sunfish was parked. Deb helped him lift it onto a roller wagon, pushing from behind as he pulled from the front. The short walk to the beach seemed longer with this awkward contraption. Deb wondered how he usually got the boat in the water when she wasn't there. She could never tell if he was frail or hardy. He seemed glad for the help. Dragging the boat, his skinny white legs looked whiter in the water. His big triangular head, gray fluff sticking out like an owl's crown, turned to Deb with constant instruction as she got in the boat and later as they sailed. This was not at all calming to Deb, as his instructions and explanations seemed not those of a captain but a swimming instructor. Deb had not liked swimming lessons as a child. But the water was calm and warm, and Jim/dad was cute in his way. She could see he was enjoying the outing, so she tried to relax and enjoy it too.

Once past the shallow pebble-bottomed waters, steady waves took the tiny Sunfish up and down as if it were on a carousel. This seemed not to bother Jim/dad, but Deb felt a little green. She tried not to show it. Apparently, she was successful, because Jim/dad just kept going further out as if all were well. Deb quietly hung on. Then a blue whirlpool sucked the boat under the water, cold and deep. Deb and the boat spat up just outside the tugging waters that had wrestled them. She climbed aboard, looking for Jim/dad. The sea was calm, except for a small area where Jim/dad was waving furiously and smiling. What was happening? Was he waving in a friendly way or drowning in panic? He seemed strong since he was not going under, but could he get out of the churning water's hold? Feeling alone, she closed her eyes and screamed, "Mah-mm!" her long-note call for help from beyond. Soon, small crafts surrounded Jim/dad, who was dog- paddling with strained effort now. They pulled Jim into Grace's boat and she threw a large towel around him. The other boats drifted apart and disappeared. Only the papyrus long boat remained with Grace, Rescue Man, Jim/dad, and a crew of paddlers. The angry spot in the sea closed up and the crew paddled in unison, delivering Jim/dad back to his granddaughter. He shivered in the striped towel, pink, purple, and yellow.

"Are you all right? How do you feel?" Deb asked.

"I feel like I'm gonna die, my heart is beating too fast," he complained.

"He's fine, the man doesn't know pain,"

Grace commented to Deb as if Jim couldn't hear. That was a curious thing to say concerning a formerly suicidal man. Perhaps she meant ALL men knew nothing of pain since her reference point for great pain was childbirth. At any rate, Grace's sympathy seemed lacking.

"I'll bring them to shore. The crew can take you on to Iceland," the man who had rescued Jim offered.

Grace nodded, ready to turn back to her course.

Deb said, "Wait! I'm looking for Dezy, do you know where he is?"

"If you're looking for him, he'll turn up. He always does," she said as the crew paddled her away. She gave a parting bemused look to her once familiars, raising her hand in a regal pose before twice curling her fingers in a small shy wave. They were gone much quicker than you would think in the small human-powered boat, speeding with great intention toward Grace's destination. Jim/dad had fallen asleep in his giant towel, curled in the pit of the boat with a life jacket pillow. Rescue Man was not very talkative and Deb was glad. She was sulking that the whole trip was a waste, and she worried about Jim/dad. The surrogate parents were no help. "He'll turn up." What infuriatingly lame advice.

Once home, Jim/dad enjoyed being the star of a true-life adventure story for weeks afterward. He enjoyed having people ask after his health since his harrowing ordeal. It was worth being a fool to know people cared.

CHAPTER 11

The next day was Sunday. The sun had just come up, but Charles was already getting dressed.

"Do you want an egg this morning?" he asked.

"Yes, thanks, and could you put on some tea water?"

"I already did."

"Good, good."

Even at top speed, Deb took a lot longer than Charles to be ready for the day. She had to sit with her tea, do her stretches, and remember her dreams. She had to wash her face, brush her teeth, and figure out her clothes; plus she ate slowly. She didn't just jump into her clothes and go. It was a process.

Today, they had plans to go out.

"Did I tell you that this evening before dark, I have to shoot a car-chase scene in the graveyard? It's for school," Deb said.

"Don't worry. We'll be back in time for you to do your homework, though it doesn't seem right for you to work on slacker Sunday."

"We're going to use toy cars. It was Tim's idea. He thought my report was boring."

"It's good to be open to other people's ideas, Deb. He can help make this report of yours more appealing to younger audiences."

"It's not my report. It's a collaborative project," Deb said, pronouncing it "co-laab-bortive."

"You sound upset. Are you ready to share your ideas or not, Deb?" Charles asked, holding her shoulders and looking her in the eye.

She stuck out her lip and put her head on his shoulder. "I'm not upset, really. Just a little irritated. I'm not used to the collaborative process anymore."

"It'll be OK. It's good to challenge yourself. People work collaboratively every day without getting blown up."

"You don't need to reassure me. I just want to make sure we don't stay too long at this event."

"I see that look on your face when you say 'collaborative.' We are going to have a nice big breakfast, your favorite with potatoes and onion. Don't be nervous. Everything is going to go just fine."

Deb sighed deeply and took a spoonful of honey, fully accepting that breakfast was going to make everything OK. Charles had that effect on her. Little anxieties vanished in their shared life.

After breakfast, they went to church. They weren't churchgoers generally, but the Lecturing Ladies were talking on a subject that was relevant to Deb's Crisis Averted project. The lecture was "The Good Book and the Fate of the Publishing

Industry," and there would also be music and special guest performers. It didn't sound church-like to Deb, but she hadn't been to church in a very long time. Some of the Lecturing Ladies were religious, and this connection between the Bible and all other books seemed like a perfect fit for a Christian venue.

Maxine and Ruby were sisters and had always been Baptists. Ruby sang in the choir, and people still spoke fondly of Maxine's late husband, Frank. Deb and Charles were hoping to have a chance to dance. They had been dancing together for a long time, and if there was good dancing music, this afternoon could be the perfect slacker Sunday. They both liked being active, but Deb liked to do things just for fun. Dancing would satisfy them both, if the car-chase scene wasn't too much for Deb.

It was only because Ruby and Maxine were members that Deb found out a man billed as "The Witness" would perform, along with other gospel groups that Sunday. Ruby advised her to bring her dancing shoes and was already gathering pink, fuzzy, sparkly items for her own outfit.

Later, the minister gave a brief appearance at the pulpit. Though there was no police force or any other governmental department, he served as the what's-up man in town. Today, he gave over the entire service to The Witness, the Can You Hear Me

Gospel Group, and the Lecturing Ladies.

While the minister made announcements at the pulpit, Deb found her eyes wandering to an alcove with a sculpture of a religious figure. She stared, lulled to stillness by a hulk of impression-less visual static. Then the figure walked off, and out the back door.

He knew before she did that she had seen him, and seen deeply enough to know that they were the same. He felt the gentle prodding of her eyes, unable to break from her gaze until his camouflage was undone. She didn't know he was her father. What she knew was, we are all the same; what she felt was an automatic reaching, a connection that came inevitably from waiting and watching. She had seen The Witness and his name was Dezy. He was old now, about seventy-four, nothing like the man she had imagined as her father all these years.

He was dressed like a spiffed-up farmer with black suspenders, white button-down shirt, and a tawny gray beard halfway down his chest. He moved gracefully for a rather large, still handsome old man. His every gesture seemed drawn out and gave dramatic edge, authority, and humor to his bearing. Dezy took the lectern in his dolphin-like hands and, leaning over it, said nothing for a while. The congregation waited in silence. Then he stood back and sort of snorted, opened and closed his mouth several times before the flow of words began in a rhythmic, almost singing voice. Addressing the congregation, he began:

"I have not always been a Christian, or even a good person. I've done some shameful things. Some of them, they break my heart to this day, and others I am not sorry for still. I'm not going to tell you what I've done, and worse, what I've not done. I know better than to try to wash others with my own bathwater. What I've come here to share today is my testimony of the living Christ."

The choir behind him broke out in a jazz jam; short bass bursts on the "ba" in bathwater, and the sopranos taking "water" in waves to the top. Dezy ignored this and went on seriously with his testimony. The choir, looking disappointed, sat down.

"What is God? Does anybody here know?"

"No God but God," a woman sang out.

"The Bible says he is the light, the love, and the way. Have you seen him?"

"Show us the way!" someone in the congregation shouted.

"It only takes one person to see the light. If one person sees it, then other people will look for it, and see it and share the way of finding it. That is how a new reality is born."

He continued, "In my darkest hour, I ran, and ran, and ran. I did not see a thing. No dark, no light, no love, no way. I literally went blind with grief. I was reduced to a man of very little means. My wife died in childbirth, and I did not even have the courage to look at my child. I became a blind wanderer. I could still play my banjo, and I could still hear echoes of my wife's voice backing me up as I sang, but I lived in darkness. The first thing I saw after many years was the darkness itself. I had lived with it for so long without seeing it. Darkness was a kind of revelation to me. It made me want to see the world again. So I sought to see again, at least in my imagination, at least in my mind. Oddly enough, that is what led me back to the church. I learned to read the Bible in Braille; it was the only book I could come by in Braille. I liked to read about miracles, and I believe that is what cured my blindness, this instruction if you will on how to let God touch and heal me. That is what the Good Book means to me. God is the way."

"God is the way," the congregation whispered in unison.

Deb had difficulty even looking at a Bible. She preferred The Gita and The Rita. She would have felt more comfortable with incense and chanting in Sanskrit. Though this church was familiar, it was also unfamiliar. It was Christian, like the Presbyterian church she was forced to go to when she was young, yet it was different. It was loud, funny, friendly, sincere, and not at all boring. The choir was rocking, and The Witness had a lot up his sleeve. Charles, she could tell, was waiting patiently for the end of the "sermon," which in his mind, you would pretty much have to be Christian to appreciate, and he was not.

"God came to me like a feather of light out of the darkness. This little feather danced its fall to earth and painted my entire world in glory and lifted me from a terrible sadness that was crushing my soul. It didn't happen so long ago. It takes time to see the light. It takes time to adjust to the mysterious presence of God's love. God is the way, God is the light, and God is the mysterious presence of love. All I did was invite him in. Have you invited God into your life?"

An encouraging shout came from somewhere in the back: "Walk with me, Jesus!"

"I'm here to tell you that miracles can happen overnight, but the deepest miracles happen a little bit every day, so keep your walk with God, invite him into your life every day. That's my testimony."

The choir piped up with a celebratory, "Every day, every day, every day!" and The Witness walked off.

"I'm not sure that's what it says in the Bible," Maxine whispered.

"Well, you haven't read it in Braille," Ruby whispered back.

Ruby had been seeing Dezy for a few months, but this was the first time her friends had seen him, and she wasn't ready to admit she had a man. It was a difficult subject to bring up in a group of widowed old women who depended on each other, a group in which men were a thing of the past. She didn't want to upset the balance. And anyway, Dezy had a secret, and her friends could not keep secrets. We all have something we aren't ready to face, and Dezy had a right to face Deb in his own way.

Deb didn't seem to notice how The Witness's testimony fit like a missing piece in her own story. Ruby hoped that Dezy and Deb would reunite, but that was not for her to manage. Dezy had been nervous, knowing that Deb was in the congregation. He kept looking off to his left, far above the heads of the crowd.

Ruby loved her sister, but Maxine was getting crankier; she needed more help because of her Parkinson's. Maxine seemed to be pushing her away lately. Ruby had always wound herself protectively around her sister even though she was only three minutes older. They were about as different as two twins could be. Their other sister, Ginny, was just three when she died in Maxine's arms. Ruby had stayed home with Mother and was not in the car accident. It could be experiences like that that made two people so different. Ruby was expansive, with lots of friends, whereas Maxine kept her life confined to a few people and hobbies.

The minister took the pulpit again. "Thank you, Witness. The witness is from the South originally and has been traveling around playing his banjo for some time, I understand. Of course, he eventually found our little paradise on earth and has been settling into the area. Please welcome De-ah-Witness, who will be playing some of his Bible ballads on his banjo downstairs. But for now, stay right here: the Lecturing Ladies will give a panel discussion on 'The Good Book and the Fate of the Publishing Industry.' I apologize to all you newcomers who may not have expected a marathon Sunday, but sometimes you have to strike while the iron is hot, and it so happens we are blessed with many opportunities this week. The policy of the church is to accept and incorporate all gifts, so long as we are able to use them in a God-willing way. There will be refreshments, music, and dancing downstairs after the lecture. There are pencils and papers in the pews if you'd like to take notes."

A long table was brought out and covered with a white cloth. The pulpit was moved to one side. Vases of flowers were rearranged. The Lecturing Ladies had a way of doing panel discussions; sort of like a cross between a filibuster and a relay. One would just start talking on a subject until she had nothing more to say about it. Then the talking stick was passed and one of the others would take the stand for a while. This would go on until there was nothing else to say on the subject; like a jam session with a lesson.

Irene took the stand and got the subject rolling. Since she was the oldest, she usually went first. It was her house they all lived in. Betty would be next, and would keep it brief. Ruby and Maxine were mixers, playing different sides of the issue. The three of them sat at the table, listening and watching for the transfer of the talking stick.

"The Bible was the first book ever published. You could say it was the guinea pig of Johannes Gutenberg's printing press. Never before had the process of spreading the word been so automatic. Before, scribes reproduced each word, each phrase, each paragraph in longhand, with nibs dipped in ink. Often these were decorative, illuminated manuscripts. Once publishing became the reproductive organ of the living word, scribes were released from their duties. Perhaps they became writers, or maybe they took up the Crusades instead."

Irene handed off the stick to Betty, who stood up and said:

"The Bible may have given life to the printing press, but it also gave it free will."

Betty pushed the stick past Ruby to Maxine, who broke out a speedy timeline:

"Oh yes, all manner of things were printed after that: magazines, newspapers, the Encyclopedia Britannica. Then came lithography for high-quality printed images, the steam- powered printing press, and a mechanical typesetting device, the whole thing improving all the while as more diverse forms of literature joined the experiment. Noah Webster published the *American Dictionary of the English Language*. In 1845, paperbacks were introduced to America. The following year, the first rotary press allowed publishers to increase circulation ten million-fold. Publishing, let's not forget, is the business of commercial production and issuance of literature. So this meant money. And where there is money, there is copyright. Paperbacks in the United States suffered near extinction due to the International Copyright Act of 1891, prohibiting the reprinting of English titles in paperback form. Meanwhile, William Morris and his Kelmscott Press set about improving the quality of books in England, with his signature high-quality illustrations and typography. Somehow, that issue must have been resolved. Perhaps the American magazine *Bookman*'s list of 'books in demand' helped pave the way."

With that, she shrugged the stick over to Ruby, who played with the stick a moment before taking a deep breath, widening her eyes, and pursing her lips in a downward smile.

"The first real literature was Beatrix Potter's *Peter Rabbit* story. Like the Bible, *Peter Rabbit* took on moral issues such as: Is it really wrong to steal? Are our moral ideals suited to our natural being? Can we really condemn Peter for eating the farmer's carrots and running away? Is he not expressing exactly what a rabbit is? Then how suitable are the Ten Commandments to the nature of a human being? Beatrix Potter had the genius to realize that to answer this question, all that was needed was to put the rabbit in human clothes, then presto, the situation was clear, thou shalt not steal!"

With that bit of clarity, Ruby got up and gave the talking stick back to Irene.

"And with zeal the muckraking began. Social critics like Upton Sinclair brought on *The Jungle*. And the Bible, the one Good Book, became many good books. Good books, bad books, and mediocre books abounded. In order to distinguish a good book from the rest, the Pulitzer Prize committee was assembled. With the rapid and profuse reproduction of works of art came the doppelganger. Within the copy machine and later the home computer, the doppelganger had a permanent home in the house of publishing. The doppelganger is a false good book, a false god, a world of mirrors, and a virus."

She passed the baton to Betty:

"Students created what they called the living word, on iPads and other tablets. They scanned their textbooks and created electronic copies that were constantly being added to and changed by its readers. They thought it was the living word. The only problem was that it wasn't. It was the doppelganger, a shadow of the living word, a clone, and a world of mirrors with no reality. This was the culmination of the publishing industry's journey into and out of being."

Betty pushed the stick past Ruby over to Maxine:

"John 14:6, Jesus answered, 'I am the way, the truth, and the life. No one comes to the Father except through me.' The word is creation, God's thoughts materialized. Any creation not based on nature or God's Eden is not even a shadow of the real thing. False worlds are a distraction from the true way, beginning with creation, leading to the creator, and then to becoming cocreators. Stepping out of this order, we miss the boat. For lack of spiritual milk — for literature is a spiritual art —publishing has starved. The publishing industry lost its way and became as worthless and inflated as the dollar. Books became fatter and fatter and sold for less and less."

On this sad note, Maxine passed the talking stick to Ruby:

"I remember when a new book would come out, it was so exciting. I grew up on *Harry Potter*; I read every one of them as soon as the next in the series came out. If literature is a spiritual art, I don't think we should give up on it. I think we just have to live with this question: How can we bring books back out of the darkness of false gods and into the light of true creation, living words coming through living worlds? How can we find the way?"

The stick was pushed around for a while, but it was clear the Lecturing Ladies had nothing more to say. Until Irene said, "Let us all find our way downstairs then for herbal tea and music." Single file, the ladies made their way from the stage and through the aisles, leading the way to the cool, dark lower level of the church.

Charles and Deb wasted no time taking the dance floor the moment they heard music fast enough to swing to. They got in two good dances before The Witness got to his "Bible Ballad," a slow one, only fit for waltzes. Ruby would have liked waltzing, but her partner was the music man at the moment. So the three of them sat it out together at a table, sipping chamomile tea, listening.

> Jacob, oh Jacob,
> Where are you moving now?
> Your whole life on a caravan of camels,
> Walking with your great flocks of sheep and goats.

> I'm going back to the land where the Lord said he would make me prosper!

> Jacob, oh Jacob,
> What fear has crept into your heart?
> You can't buy forgiveness, Jacob, what have you done?

> I have no peace with my brother visiting.
> I've long cheated Esau and now he comes no doubt to kill me.
> My God, what am I to do?

Dear God, remember me,
Remember that you promised me
My children would be as many as the stars.

An angel stepped out of the darkness.
What do you want? Jacob said.
I want to help you just as you asked! The
spirit replied.
Go away! Go away, I don't need you at all.

But the angel took him by the collar and said,
Without me you'd have nothing.
Go away! Leave me alone, Jacob said.
And wrestled the angel to the ground.

You need me, the angel said, it was you who
asked for my help.
I don't care, just leave me alone.
All right then, the spirit said, and began to
pull away.

Jacob, oh Jacob,
He wouldn't let go the angel.
Not until you bless me, Jacob said.
And they wrestled through the night.

The angel gave him the God juice right in
his hip,
To remind you of your new name.
Be known as 'he who has wrestled with

God' from now on.
Know that God is always with you, in all that you do,
and you shall be blessed.

It was one of Jim/dad's favorite Bible stories, and he had told it to her as a child before tucking her into bed. She looked at The Witness, and wondered what his real name was, because no one was really called The Witness, not every day by everyone.

An obvious truth settled on Deb: *The witness is Dezy, my real dad.*

Suddenly she felt embarrassed for him. He was like a tree cut down, sick and diseased with no family to make use of the wood. He made a profession of displaying his wounds. She felt more like a field scientist pondering the speculative existence of an extinct family of humanoids than his daughter. It was sad, and since she *was* his daughter and not a field scientist, the sadness was wholly her fault. The sick tree belonged to her.

Dezy, as if realizing his secret was freed in the song, stepped out from his banjo and started across the dance floor, making his way to Deb, Charles, and Ruby. He couldn't face Deb, so he stuck out his hand for Ruby, and they waltzed to the same song without the words. The Can You Hear Me Gospel Chorus picked it up, humming while tapping drums and bells. Dezy and Ruby moved with beautiful regularity, like a ballerina in a music box; they clicked in slow circles like magical children in their sweet wonderland. Yet they possessed a consistency in every gesture that was in keeping with their real ages and skill.

Irene was sitting at a table helping people to make tiny books from one piece of paper.

"Fold it into quadrants. Now open the quadrant so that its length is horizontal. Next, fold the two ends toward the center so that you end up with a strip of four little rectangles. Notice the middle two rectangles? Use your pencil to mark the horizontal fold of the two center rectangles. Make a cut along that line, cutting off or cutting through the fold in the middle two sections. Now pull the fold open like a diamond-shaped mouth and smush it closed. There is one page sticking out. You want to fold it over to join the other pages and make a book," she explained.

Deb made a book and used it to make a note for Dezy. She picked up a pink crayon and wrote on the cover, "Dear Dad." Then, switching to pencil, she wrote on the next page, "Sorry I couldn't stay. I had to do my homework. Mom gave me enrollment in high school for my birthday." She turned the page, wondering what to say next. Finally, she wrote: "Maybe you can help me later with another assignment. We are supposed to interview an elder in our family and write a history. You can contact me through Ruby. She knows where I live." She made the assignment up, of course, but it sounded like the kind of assignment one might get in school. She turned to the last page and, wanting to fill each page with consistency, picked up the pink crayon and wrote, "Love, Deb."

She took the note up to the stage and wove it between the strings of Dezy's idle banjo.

Returning to Charles, she said, "Let's go. It's getting late and I still have a car chase to do."

"Well, we were lucky to get in a couple of dances right off," he said. "Sounds like they're on a slow streak now."

"Yup. I guess the Lecturing Ladies will be out late tonight. They know how to waltz. We should learn it too, Charles. We may not be able to swing forever."

"No, Deb, we can swing forever, I'm sure. What's hard is learning something new."

"Well, you can't always help learning something new. Sometimes the light comes on, you get the word, and there's nothing you can do about it."

"Did some important information come in tonight? Something at the lecture? Or the dance?"

"I'm not sure yet; I have to focus on what's next. I'll comb through the lecture later."

She didn't want to deal with Dezy right now, and she didn't want Charles to rush her into some kind of emotional family reunion. *It's best if I just treat him like any other source of information for my book.* She said nothing about The Witness or Dezy.

CHAPTER 12

The next day, Deb came home to visitors. A flying carpet, rolled up into a tube shape, leaned against the door, but inside she found no one. Outside she heard a robin's urgent whistling. She scanned the view, her eyes settling on a pink blotch in the distance. Near the well, up the rocky hillside into the woods, she could make out three figures half-hidden in lush green forest. She could make out Charles's white hat, and she guessed the other two were Ruby and Dezy.

She snuck back inside before they saw her, began making tea, and went over the questions she would ask Dezy: Was our family in Hurricane Betsy? What was that like, how did Jim handle it? What was it like to have Jim as a dad? Maybe Jim had been a different person back then? She felt oddly jealous of Dezy for having known "her father" when he was a young man. It seemed she had no appropriate feelings for Dezy, given the situation: reuniting with her birth father. Dezy was just a stepping-stone to Jim. It was hard to include him in her idea of family, the family she had always known.

She wanted some munchies to settle her nerves and keep her on task with the interview, but there was nothing on hand. She licked a spoonful of honey and dipped it into her chamomile tea. The gang was approaching: Ruby, looking sweet in pink, her once red hair transitioning to white; Dezy, taking smooth strides beside her; and Charles, giving them the tour, apparently unaware of who Dezy was.

Deb offered them tea. Ruby took out her knitting, waiting and listening to see what would happen between father and daughter. Dezy just waited for whatever was meant to unfold from Deb's hospitality, like a child.

"This tea tastes like flowers," he commented.

"It's chamomile. Chamomile is the flower you saw growing at the top of the hill," Deb said.

"Wildflowers," he said.

"I suppose they are," Deb said.

"Wildflowers are my favorite kind of flower. I remember walking with Dad as a child, out by the newly constructed ranch houses in St. Bernard Parish where no one yet lived. There was a trail leading there, and I saw these amazingly delicate and varied flowers I had never seen before. I asked Dad what they were called, and he said 'wildflowers,' so I've always thought that wildflowers are my favorite," Dezy said.

"Yes, but there are many kinds of wildflowers, once you get to know them. I love columbines, bleeding hearts, and daisies. Jim/dad and Grace always grew daylilies and zinnias. I loved those, too," Deb said.

"I remember black-eyed Susan. That was one wildflower Dad taught me the name of. Haven't seen those in a while, though . . . So, you want to talk about the weather?" he asked.

"Yes, specifically Hurricane Betsy," she said.

Ruby sipped her tea slowly, while Deb and Dezy seemed to go cup after cup, reaching for their cups as if grasping at tree limbs to slow their descent into an acknowledgment neither of them exactly wanted.

Deb wasn't entirely sure she trusted him. The old man seemed innocent and dishonest at the same time; he was both wide-eyed and shifty-eyed, like an insecure cowboy. He threw every question Deb tossed him over to Ruby, who only smiled, nodded, and kept knitting. This seemed to give him courage.

He told a joke about three strings who just turned eighteen and wanted to get a drink in a bar. This was back when it was illegal to sell liquor to minors. The first two strings went into the bar and asked for a drink. They were both kicked out, and told: "We don't serve strings here." So the third string went in to try and rise above the insulting discrimination. He knew he had to do something different, so he thought up a disguise. He scratched himself up so that his fibers were all ruffed out, tied himself in a knot, and untwisted his ends. "Ohh, you look bad now!" his companions said. The bartender tilted his head, scrutinizing him a long time until finally, he said, "You're one of those strings, aren't you?" The string replied, "Frayed knot."

Dezy kept going off on little tangents like that, but Deb just kept bringing him back to Jim, New Orleans, and Hurricane Betsy.

Deb liked the joke; something about being asked to empathize with a string appealed to her. But she had little patience for puns.

Ruby looked around in desperation; it seemed the interview was about to fizzle in some sort of generation gap.

"Does this guitar still work?" she asked, plucking it off the wall. "Mind if Dezy gives it a try?"

"Oh, that, I've never played it. It belonged to an old boyfriend who left it with me. I always thought it was pretty, handmade in Hawaii. I'd love to hear somebody play it," Deb answered.

Dezy began tuning, a waterfall of sounds that put everyone at ease, most importantly himself. He seemed to be using it to pace himself. He strummed a few chords and waited for someone to speak, by this manner developing a rhythm of conversation. A few picked notes seemed to bring his memory back, allowing him to answer Deb's questions without needing to turn to Ruby.

"Did you actually leave when Hurricane Betsy came? What time of day or night was it? Were you upset or even aware of what was going on?" Deb

153

asked.

Dezy took a deep breath and looked away for a minute, trying to gather his concentration. Then he came out with a musical prologue, a dramatic scattering of tremolo notes and a single roll stroke.

"After Dad's crisis, when I was still a baby, long before Hurricane Rob came along, Hurricane Betsy slammed into low-lying St. Bernard Parish. The school where Dad taught was dismissed early for evacuation. We were renting a duplex on Linda Lou Drive, not as fancy as it sounds. It was located a long way from the city. Both Mom's and Dad's parents urged us to get out. Dad's parents, Nana and Poppa, who died before you were born, arranged for us to stay in New Orleans, as New Orleans was considered safe," Dezy said, as if remembering the words to an old song.

"So you left St. Bernard and headed for New Orleans . . . When did you all return, and what was that like?" Deb prodded.

"It was about ten days before Dad returned to our apartment to clean up after the receded floodwaters. Our neighbors, the du Plessisses, never left, took a rowboat to Poydras for shelter. Their car and home flooded, and they were well into getting cleaned up by the time Dad returned. Mr. du Plessis hosed off his recently submerged car and got it started! Our apartment was covered with mucky sediment, the walls stained up to three or four feet, furniture ruined, clothes hanging in the closet mud-stained from the floodwaters."

"How did this affect Jim/dad and were you afraid?" Deb asked.

"The water heater was closeted outside the kitchen door and choked with mud. I was unaware of the dangers. It was all the same to me, a trip to Nana and Poppa's for me. Dad gained confidence fixing the water heater. Mom returned home after the place was habitable, although practically unfurnished. I stayed at Nana and Poppa's in New Orleans a while longer."

"Tell me more about how it affected Jim/dad," Deb said.

"Well, in the aftermath of the flood, Jim began to feel cured of his misery. Hurricane Betsy was a great equalizer. Everyone was in the same boat, faced with physical tasks. Dad learned that his neighbors cared about him and that he cared about them. Things like fixing the water heater and cleaning the mud away from everything gave him confidence. He realized he could do without things. Life returned to the basics. The flood took the edge off, made him feel he had a personality he could use. Everything that almost washed away became clearer, home and family. He had a common experience with people in St. Bernard. All the special Louisiana experiences became more important, things like the pyramid-shaped crab nets they'd set in the water and pull up later for dinner, going out in the canoe, and going to the Orange Festival in Plaquemines,"

Dezy answered.

"How do you know all this?" Deb asked, amazed.

"I was like our family historian, I always had an ear for stories that I would make into songs," Dezy said.

"Wherever you go, there you are, as Jim/dad used to say."

"Yup, he used to say that, all right. He was always getting us lost on those family trips Mom planned, the Triple A maps all over the place," Dezy said. "In all my wandering, all the things I remember, my debts, my sins, unpleasant flashbacks from my life, I've made peace with all that. What bothers me is the part I was too young to remember, and stuff that happened before I was born. All this history was passed down to me. I sing the songs, but I don't remember those times. I imagine them from a child's point of view. When I was young, sometimes I would remember something we used to have, and when I asked Mom and Dad where it was, what happened to it, they would say, 'That must have disappeared in the flood.' "

"I've wondered what the drive was like as the family left St. Bernard for the safety of New Orleans," Deb said.

"I was too young to remember, but I had a dream about that recently."

"Tell me the dream."

Dezy began to strum the guitar, thinking about

156

it. At first, a dreamy, flowing melody came. Then he broke into "I Wish I Was in Dixie" before returning to a slower song, "Red River Valley."

"I didn't even know Dad was there: no one did till I pointed out a sound, something like a song coming from the front dash of the car. The more Mom and I listened and tried to locate it, though, the clearer the song became until at last Jim just appeared, playing his harmonica in the front seat of that old Rambler we used to have. As soon as it was obvious that the sound was Dad, Mom seemed to calm down as if this were one of our regular outings—though the water was rising to curb level outside, and the rain was unremitting."

Dezy continued, "I loved the sound of Dad's harmonica, I always did. Dad would say he learned such things in the Navy. 'An old trick I learned in the Navy,' he used to say. That was one of Dad's witticisms. Dad was never cut out for war. He was too willing to sacrifice his life without accounting for what the Stars and Stripes would get for it. He was ready to throw his blood away as if it were ketchup in a movie. That's what Dad was like as a young man."

Deb bristled at hearing Dezy refer to Jim/dad and Grace as Mom and Dad. It gave her the odd feeling that Dezy was like a brother to her instead of a father. She was also jealous of the time he had spent in New Orleans, before it was lost to the Mississippi Sea.

"Dad told me," Dezy said, "that after the incident where he threw the book in church, and the Buckleys took us into their friendship, he felt for the first time that he was angry and unhappy and he was still OK. All that shit, excuse me, in the South was hard for Dad. He was a naive idealist in the city of sin, witnessing some pretty unfair treatment of his fellow men: racism, homophobia, et cetera. But in the end he came to understand that in the South, people didn't express everything they felt. Deep down, though, people understood there was some basis of change."

It felt as if she was trying to solve a mystery that didn't exist. Sometimes the only clue she had was the urge to search for meaning in Jim's crisis.

She thanked Dezy for the interview, cleared the dishes, and showed them out the door, but the wild boar was standing there. Dezy and Ruby were afraid to go near it. Dezy had seen wild boars but never up close like this.

"Don't worry about the boar. I'll get him to move with this compost. Come on, Jeezum." Deb took a bucket from under the counter and led the wild boar away to a shady hillock.

Dezy and Ruby were amazed, and this might have been how the unfortunate rumor spread about Deb having a pet pig. At any rate, they were leaving now, but not before Dezy made the awkward gesture of putting his arm around Deb, congratulating her on her "first celebrity interview." She was sickened both by the physical closeness and the stupid joke. He, her supposed father, did not know anything about her, or life in general. She felt she had found something of uncertain worth in her father. *I mean, who needs this humbling?*

Ruby spoke up, breaking the awkward moment, "You'll have to have Dezy back. He knows more than he told you today, little things that will help you understand."

"Thanks, I will, and you two can stop by anytime, you know that." Deb's natural generosity was restored once Dezy backed off and Ruby intervened. After all, he was her father, and she didn't like the ambivalence she felt about him.

There are always people who comb through everything, sensitive people who would know if they had been pricked by an unacknowledged reality sleeping in a haystack. It's the feeling of transition, the knowledge that at certain temperatures we melt; we transform into something else, not quite ourselves.

The heat wave of the last few days had only somewhat relented, and Deb had to hit the couch before figuring out what to make for dinner. As she drifted off, she thought, *there are basically two ways I could go for dinner. I can live in the present and eat wild food from the land; I can gather milkweed*

159

blossoms and batter them up and fry them like Irene taught me to do. Or I can live in the past and consult our pantry of scavenged relics. Everybody had a stash of looted groceries, goods of the factory-made type that were long ago discontinued. You couldn't live on this out-of-date, dinted-can food, but it helped fill the gaps in what they could gather and make edible from what was left of nature. They'd eat that crutch out from under themselves soon. Morally, they couldn't eat meat; no one could. Until people earned forgiveness from the animals, they wouldn't return in great numbers. In Middleburg, it was as if everyone had given up meat for Lent, a Lenten time that had lasted at least ten years, maybe more. Even if the feeling had been otherwise, there simply were not enough animals to make hunting or keeping livestock feasible. Humans had the thinnest thread connecting them to a continued future. Flowers, nature's vital reproductive organs, and honeybees, the pollinating love messengers, still gave hope of an earthly comeback.

When Charles returned, they decided after much discussion on the obvious: spaghetti. They had a half-eaten jar of spaghetti sauce to use up; Deb had forgotten about that.

As she watched the water boil over the new "rocket" stove Charles had constructed out of twelve clay bricks, Deb was drawn into a drama unfolding on the water's skin. An amoeba of oil undulated on top of the water. *"It has a thick skin of shadow around its yellow body. It changes as the water gets hotter. It's moving. I throw a pinch of salt in the pot, and the water speeds its turning. The blob is getting very skinny in the middle. Can the sunflower oil sustain oneness? Will there soon be two shadow-skinned selves? Finally, it breaks. The small one is born. Victorious! Wonderful! But what will happen next? The two circle round, sometimes coming dangerously close. Until finally, it happens: the pot is too small, the universe is not infinite for the sunflower oil constellations. The little one has no place else to go but—disgusting! What a betrayal! The little one has merged back into the belly of the big one—back—when they touch, they dissolve into each other."* Too impatient to see if any further realities would evolve, Deb threw the pasta in. *Wherever you go, there you are.* Perhaps the world was that small.

Charles set the timer for nine minutes as soon as he saw Deb had put in the pasta; he always liked to time it. Deb never bothered with that. She would pull out a strand for tasting when she thought it was getting close. She never heard the timer go off anyway. It just didn't get her attention somehow.

"Let's say some of the stuff is done as far as getting our homestead ready for the postapocalyptic world we are now in," Charles said. "I mean, we're late, and not as well set up as we should be for the end of the world, but the root cellar is in, we have a

161

well and a hand pump, we have our wild simulated garden, a composting toilet, an outdoor kitchen and an indoor kitchen, all the firewood we could want . . . Still, it seems we're so far away from having our house built. I don't know if we'll ever have solar power."

"The world ending is so yesterday. Instead of ending, it just slowed down a lot," Deb said.

"I just want to be ready for the worst, but I get the feeling I never will be," Charles said.

"It's the journey that counts."

"The journey to the end of the world?"

"If that's your journey, Charles, savor it. Perhaps you have a role to play, being prepared, helping others, and not panicking. Just do what you can in the time you have. Don't worry if it's not good enough," Deb said, singing the last few words.

Near the outdoor kitchen, there was a giant rock that was split in two so that there was an open path between the two parts. Moss grew on top of the rock, and it was a beautiful feature of the land they had been drawn to.

"I dreamed that an earthquake came, and we went into the split rock to be safe, but the earthquake pushed the two halves together and we got squashed," Charles said.

"Aw, how sweet. Maybe, though, if there is an earthquake, we shouldn't go to Split Rock," Deb answered.

On that note, she lit a beeswax taper and set

out the meal she'd been preparing. They sat and held hands across the table for a moment before beginning.

"Thanks for sharing this meal with me," Charles said.

"Of course."

They ate at the picnic table outside. It was still light out, but it was nice to have a little flame in sight, bringing focus to the meal.

Deb remembered how whenever something went awry, Jim/dad used to say, "Story of my life . . ." Deb never knew what he meant by that, until she was old enough to see that small pieces of life could become the lens through which you saw the whole. It came to her like the shape of a roof with everything important under it, especially family. *I am going to have to adjust my sights to Dezy. He's my actual father. He has some of the shattered mirror of Jim/dad glittering inside him.* She wondered if Charles already knew that Dezy was her real dad. Sometimes he knew things but kept them to himself, if it was something he sensed Deb didn't want to admit to.

CHAPTER 13

When the image of "respectable adult" shattered, what could be left?

Jim found a man struggling for respect and an appropriate vocation. He found this man was loved and supported, even in his struggles. Seeds of hope shook free from the folds of his agony. He found a life he could be grateful for, and realized the world was bigger than he thought.

***

Deb wasn't so sure. It wasn't that she felt trapped in her world, but it didn't seem big. In fact, just that night, it got more crowded. Charles had something to tell her.

"I hate to tell you this, Deb, but we are going to have to kill the pig."

"Why? I thought we were practically vegans, eating low on the food chain. What about all that?"

"Conflict."

"What conflict? Me and my pig were just sitting here, drinking tea and wallowing about, when you came along talking about killing and conflict."

"Listen, Deb. I've been a bee man for a long

time, and I've learned that you have to head off conflict before it arrives. You know what I'm talking about? Alfred, who lives in the green house with the guard dog; some proactive sweetening could save us a whole lot of trouble with him."

"So give him a jar of honey. You don't have to go whole hog. I'm not a killer! And he's not my pig!"

"Listen, I found out some stuff today. I was talking to him over the fence out back. His dog has a cut paw, and I gave him honey to put on the wound. The guy really appreciated it, but he was quite upset. He said that some sort of feral pig, some kind of hairy boar had gotten into his house and eaten his papers and bedsheets, and his dog had gotten hurt trying to defend him and his wife. Turns out he's the French chargé d'affaires. He's been talking to people and heard that the pig belongs to you. He wants you to kill the wild boar, Deb. I say we take advantage of nature's bounty, fatten ourselves up for the winter, and make friends with our new neighbor before this conflict goes international."

"You make it all sound so good. What about the downside, like blood and gore and death, and do you know how hard it is to kill a boar?"

"I know, Deb, I've heard, and I have the knuckles to prove it. I know you like to be comfortable, but sometimes you have to work to get there. I'm telling you, once we kill this pig and roast him up, there will be nothing but love and peace in the neighborhood. Look at yourself, Deb. You know you need the fat."

"You're talking about my friend. Do you think I'm going to help you kill him?"

"I think you're the only one who can, Deb. I'm asking you, please. Jeezum was your friend for a while; it's time to move on. Take what you learned, and reap your rewards."

"I don't know if I want to serve the French affairs of whatever he is. I've never had a good vibe from him."

"You have to make good vibes, Deb. He's a powerful man, and this is our chance to make peace, where before there were only bad vibes."

"Those are very sensible arguments, and there is something I've always wanted to do ever since we moved here."

"What's that?"

"I want to make a trap: a deep hole covered with brush to camouflage it, and in the bottom of the hole punji sticks are pointing up."

"You're so mean, Deb. I just don't understand you. First you don't want to kill Jeezum, then you think of the most torturous way of doing so."

"I'm just following my interests. I'm interested in Jeezum, but I'm also interested in punji stick traps."

"Maybe we could make a miniature punji stick trap and drop a pig doll named Jeezum into it."

"Like voodoo?" Deb asked.

"I'll do the voodoo, and you can back me up with the bow and arrow, just in case," Charles said.

"Let's open a bottle of mead and plan the party, the killing, and toast to whatever happens," Deb said.

"Whatever happens . . ." Charles said, lifting his glass.

A fingernail of moon was shining brightly as they strolled out onto their makeshift patio. Solar flashlights hung from trees over an area they had civilized by arranging stones for floor and seating. The bright moon, surrounded by rainbow light, was a perfect example of the strange kind of vision Deb was having lately.

"Try my glasses and see if you can see a rainbow around the moon."

Charles tried on her glasses, and he could see the rainbows around the moon and even around the solar lights. Deb showed him how the lenses of her glasses had a subtle crackled effect like crazed glaze on pottery.

"You should get that fixed," he said. "It could be hurting your eyes."

"It's too expensive to get fixed. Besides, I like my rainbow vision."

Believing that somehow she was special because she could see rainbows, delusions of grandeur threatened her objectivity. She wondered: Did these glasses allow her to see something that was really there, only not visible to the naked eye? A microscope didn't make things up; it just revealed what was too small to see. Or did these glasses actually produce an illusion? Did they make her see things that weren't there?

She had on occasion seen the rainbow light without her glasses. In the old days, when she was traveling, staying in a hotel, she got out of the shower and saw rainbow light all around herself. It seemed to enlarge in the steam from the hot shower. The way you might run your hand through water and watch the ripples created, Deb enjoyed playing with the rainbow light, hanging in the air like a big fuzzy outline around her body. This was proof that it was not just the glasses that caused the rainbow light.

Her glasses had changed over time: the lens coating that made the glasses turn dark in the sun had cracked due to overly high temperatures. But even when she first got the glasses, she noticed that she could look into the sky and find rainbows in the clouds, subtle rainbows, and if she pointed these out to other people, they were able to see them too. The rainbows always got brighter when people noticed them. Perhaps it was the dimming effect of the sunglasses that allowed Deb to look in a relaxed way into the bright areas of the sky, and thus rainbows became more visible.

As soon as you heard a pig's cries, you were sorry. In theory, Deb thought that hunting for food was a good idea, the right thing to do, but the bluckedy-bluck of the aftermath and the sadness of taking a life had prevented her from stepping into the world of the hunter.

She was trying to ease into the possibility of following in the footsteps of ancient humans who hunted for food. She would track the wild boar and get within shooting range. She would choose her weapon, a bow or a gun. She would be ready with a butchering and cooking plan to be enacted immediately after the kill. Was it possible to be a Buddhist anymore? Had she ever been one? She believed in compassion toward all beings, ahimsa. She had eaten meat at restaurants in the remote past, but she had never known any hunters. She didn't like loud noises, so she was leaning toward the bow. Perhaps some things, like eating meat, couldn't be completely resolved philosophically.

As if Jeezum knew what she was thinking, he made himself scarce. Meanwhile, Alfred's shrubberies had mud rubs and bark removed three and a half feet from the ground, suspiciously at pig height, and a wallow had formed in his front yard. He made frequent visits to ask how the pig hunt was going. Deb explained that very careful preparations were needed to "bag" such a fierce animal, who had been goring hunters since Artemis sent her monster boar to punish King Oeneus for neglecting her in his first offering of fruits to the gods.

She needed more time to gather courage

and know-how to milk this deed for all the social currency it was worth. Or at least defer further problems from the French. Apparently, the papers that Jeezum ate were very important, and Alfred had threatened war, which seemed ridiculous, but wars had been started for stupider things.

It was hard to know what the wild boar would be like under his coarse, almost sharp fur. She had much to learn about boars. She knew Jeezum was a mature male because of his tusks, but had no idea what to expect of his meat. Grace liked to shoot soda cans off a fence as a child and she was good at it too, but that was practically forgotten history. It seemed unrelated to the more civilized people they had become just two generations later.

Deb justified the hunt with the fact that she was hunting for food, yet this phrase from Jim's story kept coming back to her: "Son, you need an avocation as well as a vocation." She remembered how she used to cut the stamps off letters he sent to her, so she could send them back to him for his collection. It finally occurred to her: Jim had chosen stamp collecting as his avocation. Not painting, not poetry, not photography, but stamp collecting! She never even noticed the prescription for life he was taking. Stamp collecting was his therapy. By comparison, hunting seemed a great sport, an avocation that filled a human need much more fully than stamp collecting.

The key was to kill by surprise. If your quarry

was chased and tormented, trying to escape death, it ruined the taste of the meat. The lactic acid produced in the muscles, full of adrenaline, would taste like a bad day.

Deb dreamed of blood pouring from her boar, his body hanging from a tree. She felt her own blood drain, light-headed and faint. The next day, she found herself dry in the mouth, thirsting for ice, as she hauled wood to their fire pit. She had a headache. Slicing open a hard-crusted roll, she accidentally cut her finger. Tired, she sat down on the couch and looked at her nails. The vertical ridges seemed to say, *"I'm an anemic vegetarian losing blood."* Not the way a hunter should feel.

Deb preferred diagrams of the body, thin-lined illustrations, not the photographs she found when trying to figure out how to "dress" her boar, assuming she would shoot it with an arrow.

The trees they cut down to build their house had been giants, trees that could have easily flattened anyone unlucky enough to be in the way when the timber fell. Deb had skinned the trees so the bark wouldn't cause the wood to rot when they used the logs to build their house. The trees bled. Their sap might not be red like human blood, but it was the source and the essence of their life just the same. Deb's pants were wet and sticky with it. Just like animals killed for meat, trees had to be dressed and butchered before they went bad. You had to take care of the wood before it got stained and rotten. A couple of months on the ground and their log pile of red oak was worth nothing commercially. There was no commercial lumber now anyway, but the point still could be made. They would use the water stained logs for beams in their home of course. They were still good for that. Once you had seen the trees growing and risked your life to cut them down, in your heart, they were worth a lot more than anyone would pay for them. Plants and animals might not be so different when it came to killing and harvesting, except for the obstacle of blood and fur turning the stomach. And yet when you smelled meat cooking, it was irresistible.

The smell of something was its true knowledge, the way culinary and medicinal herbs told about themselves and influenced our mood with their scent. Deb imagined this communion of rosemary, sage, and thyme mixed with wild boar, turning over the fire.

Looking for some guidance, Deb took out her journal from last year and opened it to a random page:

> Coming out of the college library that night to go to the free movie with Charles, I noticed all the bikes lined up in the bike rack, all covered with fresh snow. They were so pretty, each perfectly high-lighted in furry snakes of snow. One lone black bike was perfectly delightful this way. I stood there admiring it, saying to Charles

it would make a beautiful picture, and I wished I had a camera in my bag. He seemed to think the wish to take a picture of ordinary bikes in ordinary snow was silly, and we walked on. Everything around us was so beautiful. Just take a look around you, I told Charles, the college is so pretty, the night so delicate, the snow so surprisingly fresh in March, it's amazing. I felt so lucky to be at this place in this time to see the ordinary wonders of an ordinary night. Just then the old- fashioned street lamps turned on. They look like antiques, yet actually they are lit with lunarflection and save the town energy. Charles said that I must be wearing my rose-colored glasses to be able to see such sights. We were going to see *Les Miserables*. We would not be eating popcorn, because all popcorn is genetically engineered. I sincerely miss popcorn.

What Charles said about "my rose-colored glasses" gives me a suspicious feeling, like I am in a world that others barely see. I try not to worry and I've gotten pretty good at it. I let go of my losses and open my heart to what avails itself to me.

I found myself laughing at the wrong time in the movie. The French guard came up to the ragtag revolutionary barricade in the street and shouted, "Who are you?"

From the top of their rampart, a child shouted back, "The French Revolution!" Immediately the guard opened fire and I burst out laughing. Somehow, the gunfire seemed like a punch line. Sadly, in real life war is no joke. Pow! Bam! Stars bursting red smoke in the air: seems such a cartoon, and I wish it were. My rose-colored glasses laugh at the blast, forgetting sad meanings and embracing light, even firecracker light.

CHAPTER 14

There was a field where everyone in high school went, a hangout spot. Cliques of girls and boys and even some grown-ups sat in circles on the ground, the ground that Robert Frost had walked on. It was a popular spot; blueberries still grew there, and teenagers were still and serious as if their futures might also come up as rare blue sapphires. They were like meditation circles, but there was a sort of gossipy teenage telepathy going on. Deb, sitting there after school one day, as if in a trance, obeyed an urge to eat the grass. It tasted like peppermint; perhaps it was a kind of peppermint. A girl who looked like Barbra Streisand offered her branches of sweet cicely, without saying a word. Of course, none of the teenagers would have even known who Barbra Streisand was. Deb thought of her as someone who was beautiful in her own way, not necessarily in society's way.

Tim belonged in the field; he wore moccasins, and he spoke the language of language. He could speak to all people because he had heart grammar, a way of grabbing onto meaning with sound. He was a eurythmic boy. In this field, that was understood. This was the field where Robert Frost pounded his poems out by foot, and the earth was still answering to this day. Vibrations once absorbed, filtered and now falling, grew new words in different orders from the same earth.

He remembered Deb sitting next to him. It was slightly embarrassing to have an older woman for a friend. She could have been his aunt or something. Some people might have thought she was his mother. Tim wasn't sure how he felt about Deb. He couldn't define it. Love is all about getting what you need. He could have sat down next to a girl his age, a pretty girl, or he could have sat next to a boy his age, but after his mother's death, Tim no longer felt connected to his peers. When your mother dies, it is alienating. Tim found the normalcy of his peers, with their push toward conformity, stifling.

Tim had only been three when his mother died, but he remembered her last gesture well. It might not have actually been her last gesture, but in Tim's memory, the very last thing that happened before she vanished was that she was tucking him into bed. It was a very hot night, and she was wrapping him in blue-striped sheets, as if he were a baby who needed to be swaddled. He was trying to get his arms and legs free; he felt like he would suffocate if confined this way. The sheets, cool at first, heated up quickly. He wanted to accept his mother's love, and he knew it might be the last time he had a chance to, but he couldn't. He just couldn't stand it. He had been a grown-up ever since.

Maybe what happens to us just exaggerates who we are, giving us a stage on which to exhibit our character. Tim found different constellations to organize his life by: his different brother and his indifferent father. And now there was Deb, who seemed not like a grown-up either. She was an odd grown-up, wise, playful, and sneaky. It was a good combination for Tim. That was why he brought her to the field. She would never have known to come here by herself, or if she had, she would have shied away. Big-brother type that he was, he brought her for her own good. Of course, she was a natural, eating the grass and forgetting all about him. Tim didn't care. He appreciated not being swaddled.

Tim felt sleepy, remembering the lyrics of "Sweet Cicely," a lullaby that his mother had made up. It was his, and no one else knew it, he was sure. But Deb got the sweet cicely.

> Sweet cicely, sweet cicely, how long have you been gone?
> Only as long as you have forgotten, I was here all along.
> What have you been under that I couldn't see your face?
> I've been under the fat lie of the fall from grace!

When will you fill my cup the way Mother used to do?

I'll fill it in the morning with sweet licorice dreams,

And if I can't remember one sweet dream my whole life through,

Then sweet cicely, then what will you do?

I'll take you on a boat ride and rock your memories out,

Until you feel so light and free that birds fly through your heart.

I will be your last bouquet, if you catch me on your last day.

My fragrance will retreat into the flashback of your life,

And you will walk on air onto the land of your delight.

The girl, oddly pretty with the bump on her nose, had walked straight to Deb and given her the sweet cicely, not him. As if Melonie preferred Deb, he couldn't help thinking. What would Deb do with the sweet cicely? Did she have any idea what it meant? Tim doubted that she did.

Feeling jealous of Deb and completely out of control, he did something he had not done in a long time. He sat and drew in his mind an arrow, and shot it to the imaginary place his mom was. A blue light appeared. It was just there for a moment, but he recognized it, like a light touch to remind him she was there in another dimension.

Deb, down from the mountain and the fields of blueberries, immediately set out to find the meaning of sweet cicely. She had been nuzzling its fragrant face of white flowers and nibbling its licorice leaves. The seedpods intrigued her, but she left them intact, despite the urge to open them and see how the seeds lined up inside. Not knowing where else to go, she went to the Lecturing Ladies and asked them what they knew about the herb. Irene took the herb and hugged it tight, saying,

"It's a shame you don't have more of it. Rare and beautiful, her face and flavor in as many variations as there were once countries."

Deb couldn't believe her stupidity in bringing all of it here, now that she saw how the old woman clutched the greens. "Here, let's put it back in the water and set it in the light so we can see it," Deb said, gently prying the greens from Irene.

Irene let them go easily once Deb spoke up and touched her long fingers. Deb's touch gave a slightly electric feel that was weakening, like a sudden realization of danger. It was a trick she had learned, a sort of negotiating skill.

Irene said she wanted to make a little tea from them, so they could taste the steeped leaves while they admired the bouquet. She asked Deb to make a fire while she got the cups and water. The other ladies started waking from their naps. "Been a long time since I've had sweet cicely," Betty said. Her voice revealed a slight distemper.

Once Deb got the fire going, she asked, "Do you have any old herb books? Just to make sure it really is sweet cicely."

"It's sweet cicely, all right. You can tell by the way it tastes, and by the way it smells. I never forget a plant like sweet cicely. You don't need a book for that," Irene said.

"Give her the book," Betty said, barely moving. When Betty spoke, you heard the words flat and plain, but you never saw her make the words; it was as if a recording of sayings came from her location.

Maxine and Ruby came out in their housecoats. Ruby had a fat dusty book in her hands, just the kind that Deb dreamed of, an answer book. Maxine shuffled badly, and took several tries to sit down in a chair where tea would be served. Ruby kept adjusting the chair to make sure it was under Maxine's bottom when she landed. Maxine kept changing her posture and reevaluating the chair. Finally, Ruby set the book before her. The book, a diary, had entries by naturalists who had pooled their knowledge and observations on every plant within their reach. There were parts of plants pressed between the pages; there were drawings and notes in many different hands.

"Let's have some seeds, Ruby," Maxine said.

Ruby pinched seeds from the plant and passed them out.

"So harmless you cannot use it amiss," commented Betty from her corner.

"It says here that the roots can be boiled and eaten with oil and vinegar, and that it's very good for old people who are dull and without courage," Maxine said.

"It rejoiceth and comforteth the heart and increaseth their lust and strength," Betty amended.

"Give me that Deep Green religion!" Maxine enthused.

Betty took a little book out from under her butt and shook it. "*The Modern Herbal*, by Mrs. Grieve," she said, quickly replacing it under her bottom.

Deb had to turn the pages of the diary carefully. There was plenty to fall from between the pages, fragile specimens, like the artist sketchbooks she used as a story wrangler many years ago. A long piece of card stock with an old postage stamp affixed to the top fell out.

"What's that?" Deb asked.

"It's called a bookmark," Maxine replied. "People used to use them back when reading books was popular to mark their place, so that they could pick up reading where they left off. Isn't it quaint?"

"Funny, I thought it was a skinny postcard. Why the stamp?" Deb asked.

"My old Frank, he collected stamps and liked to put them on things for decoration," Maxine said.

"You could do a whole lecture on bookmarks. I could find loads of people who would like to learn how to keep their place using decorative papers," said Deb.

"Sometimes they're informative, too," Ruby spoke up. "I have some that have scripture on them."

"Wow," said Betty. "I have some with recipes on them. That's really more useful, I think."

"We used to advertise our lectures with bookmarks, but we noticed that no one was noticing," added Irene.

"Not to get distracted," Maxine said, turning a page with a baggie of sweet cicely seeds taped to it. "Says here to eat six for protection against 'elf shot.' "

"What's 'elf shot'? That's ridiculous!" Deb said.

"I say we each eat six, it can't hurt," Maxine suggested.

"Maxine is a seedy lady," Irene commented. "I think the tea is taking effect."

"What are you afraid of?" Maxine asked.

"Who are you talking to?" Ruby quaked.

"I'm talking to Deb. Why did you come here? What are you really looking for? Who is after you?"

"No, no, I'm not in trouble. There was a blue light—it crossed my path. I was just looking for a story with a graceful ending, a story that would save everyone from a catastrophe, but sometimes some lives have to come to a bad end in order for others to come to a good end," Deb explained.

"Has it occurred to you that you might be

crazy?" Maxine asked.

Ruby nudged Maxine, saying, "That wasn't helpful."

"No," Deb said. "It's a valid question, but I know I'm not crazy because everything is real. There is a real pig that I'm hunting, and the story I'm looking for is the same story that all the survivors are looking for. No one talks about it and no one writes about it. But I have sleuthed the truth about a crisis that was averted. If I could find it, we could live our lives to their natural end without any disfigurement."

"Disfigurement? Is that what you are afraid of?" Maxine asked.

"There is something besides sweet cicely in this tea, Irene," Ruby pointed out.

"Just weed, male and female buds together doing their thing. Don't worry about it, Ruby. Deb is finally coughing up her goose," Irene explained.

"I'm going to become a butcher, disfiguring a fellow mammal, I'm afraid. The pig is my friend, and blood, gore, death, and loud noises are what I most want to avoid," Deb said.

"She has problems," Betty blurted.

"Butchering is not a problem," Maxine corrected. "Butchering is an old-fashioned skill that brings food to the table. You can cut out the middleman, but you can't cut out the butcher."

Ruby: "You know what? I don't think this is funny. Does everything have to be funny? One cup of tea and you lose your goddamn manners! We're talking about blood here, taking a life. Can't you have some respect?" Ruby went to the cupboard and broke out some Pop-Tarts. "Whatever," she said, vigorously cutting them up into little squares. She passed them out like Communion. The plate came to Maxine last.

"Disfigurement," she mumbled.

"I didn't plan on saying that," Deb said. "I'm not sure if we have come to the right conclusion."

"Don't worry," said Ruby. "We'll solve the problem."

A complaint came from Betty's side of the room, "Ain't no mountain high enough."

The ladies seemed to be dozing off after their snack, and Deb snuck out, avoiding good-byes. On the way out, she took a branch of her sweet cicely. She thought about trying to get that book out from under Betty's butt, but decided to leave well enough alone.

CHAPTER 15

As if it hadn't been a full enough day, Deb didn't make it home without seeing Alfred wave through his window. Without changing her pace or making eye contact, she kept on going, giving a halfhearted wave. Not that there was anything wrong with Alfred, except the threat of war with France, but Deb tried to avoid interactions with the Greenhousers. Alfred was strangely normal when he shouldn't be, and his wife smiled too much. She seemed desperately friendly. Frankly, she just didn't know what it was about them she didn't like. They looked like a model interracial couple, right out of a diversity catalogue. For some reason, she was afraid of them, especially Alfred.

Deb remembered her first encounter with Alfred, not long after she and Charles moved into the neighborhood. She was returning from one of her walks when Alfred came out to get his mail. She tried to pace herself so she wouldn't meet him, but he seemed to be timing his steps especially to greet her. He looked so clean and formal, like a dignitary.

"We're going to have a collision," Deb joked.

"That's funny," he replied without laughing.

Deb wondered if he thought she was avoiding him because he was black. He wasn't just a little black. He was so dark he was bright and shining. She sensed authority in his formal clothing and straight face. The thought that he might think that she was afraid of his color made her regret her impulsive avoiding. There had not been many people of color in Middleburg before the Great Wobble—by coincidence? Segregation was an uneasy, if secondhand, memory that hadn't faded away completely. Jim/dad and Dezy had been enmeshed in the cultural violence of a racially divided South. The lack of social freedom had hurt everyone.

No one knew exactly how he maintained the appearance of foreign authority; his story was nearly unbelievable. He said he was the French chargé d'affaires, representing French interests in Middleburg. This office hadn't existed since the West was won, yet everyone believed it. His acting was impeccable. He and especially his wife were so extroverted that their friendliness was astonishing to a quiet person like Deb.

His temperament was cool, calm, and professional as if he were from another world; he had his hair trimmed almost to the scalp, and always wore a collared shirt and tie. His facial features were smooth and unreadable. His handsome face gave no specific claim to being a certain type of person. He was able to take on many roles, Deb suspected.

She was not eager to get to know him or his wife, though she was curious about them.

"My wife told me that some new people moved in across the street," he'd said, sticking out his hand.

Why were they the new people? They had lived here before the Wobble, whereas Alfred and his wife moved in right after, into a house others had fled. Middleburg was Deb's hometown. Alfred and his wife just happened to miss their boat back to France.

Louisa was with Alfred when he left France, though their relationship was uncertain at that time. She was supposed to be his secretary; however, things evolved along different lines. She was blue-eyed and dark-haired, with pale, glowing skin and an amazing smile. The boat ride was long and boring, but Alfred tried to make it fun for her, so she wouldn't quit and so he could enjoy her smile.

Louisa felt confident when she knew how things were done. She was the opposite of Deb, who felt more confident if a general idea was enough for her to intuitively discover the rest.

One day, Louisa called out from her porch, "Good morning, Deb!" as she walked by. The woman's movie-star smile inexplicably frightened Deb. The couple showed no interest in Charles, perhaps because he didn't walk past their house. There was nothing practical in that direction.

Deb was cautious of their dog, Francesca. Francesca was a white dog; her hair was long and fluffy. Formidable in size and manner, she was always alert and acting the part of her master's servant: sometimes house guard, at other times social ambassador. It seemed she would do anything for her people.

Sometimes Francesca would trail Deb, walking along the edges of the property, and bark a slow, firm, muffled bark at even intervals. Once, she jumped the fence to follow Deb and just stood there for a moment before jumping back into her own yard.

Perhaps her distrust of the Greenhousers dated back to the time when Deb crossed into their yard, hopping the little do-nothing fence just like the dog had. She was interested in a bright orange mushroom in their yard. She could hear the dog barking from inside that day. After examining the mushroom and determining that it was a lobster mushroom, too far gone for eating, she turned back home. Later, a neighbor who lived two houses down told Charles that Alfred was upset about the trespassing, and had asked him to tell Deb to please ask permission before entering his yard.

Deb took a dislike to Alfred as soon as she heard the message about not trespassing. Maybe she'd overreacted, though. Alfred seemed kind and competent—not the worst kind of authoritative person.

It did occur to her, after giving the halfhearted

wave, that sometimes a story wrangler had to look into the things they most wanted to avoid. She silently retraced her steps and climbed into an apple tree where she could take in the view inside their kitchen.

Alfred went to his curly-haired wife, Louisa, and performed his mock butcher routine for her entertainment.

Louisa was the only one in Middleburg who knew about Alfred's past as a lowly butcher before he went into politics. She loved and longed for meat. She was pregnant and near crazy to end her craving for bacon. So to please his wife, Alfred would do these performances for Louisa, where he would take a stuffed animal belonging to Francesca and pretend to butcher it. He would talk his way through it as if teaching a course on home butchering to the layperson.

"Cutting meat is like surgery," he said. "You have to know everything before you make the first cut."

He described what he was seeing at each layer so she forgot she was looking at a stuffed animal; she was in a dream of red meat, muscle, bone, fat, and skin. The way Alfred described butchering made her imagine that everything had a place, and that things happened in order. This order reassured her that the fetus inside her would mature into a baby, and the baby would be born, and grow into a child.

He told her that when a town lost its butcher, it

forgot the natural order of things. "It loses heart," he said. Louisa did not want to lose heart; she needed to see how things were done. If she could not get a bite of meat to eat, at least she could believe that there was a process by which it could be procured, not by magic but by the hands of her husband.

Alfred brought out a tray of "headcheese samples," really just saltines, pretending they were from the stuffed lamb he'd been demonstrating the basics of butchery on.

"I like to use every part of the animal. Headcheese is a great way to use the head meat. The natural gelling agents cooked from the skull bones bring it all together in a sliceable loaf, and with a little sage and some coriander, you have a well-liked, old-fashioned party food! Voila!"

"Lovely!" Louisa said, taking three crackers, one in her right hand for now and two in her left hand for later. The crackers were part of their game. They were one of the foods that, while not adding much nutritionally, helped Louisa feel settled inside. They took the edge off the nausea that could creep up just before hunger.

"I'm going to hang these salamis up in the cellar to cure. Will you be OK for a minute?" Alfred picked up a few red socks, filled with cherry pits and sewn at the top, that Louisa liked to heat up and put behind her neck and shoulders on cold nights to help her relax.

"Those salamis look very familiar," she said.

"Oh, people always fight over salamis. I used my father's cellar once to cure salami, and he never would let me retrieve it! He acted as if it had grown there right on his property!" Alfred kept the game, the stories, the playfulness going as long as he could. The worst thing was when Louisa got bored. She once told him that the problem with men was they just weren't very fun. She said it right in the middle of their lovemaking. She was right. He was push-button boring, yet he had developed a dry and secret humor for her that he was proud of. She loved games of pretend, team spirit, and wit. When he couldn't muster a shred of entertainment, he tried to resist interacting at all, before he said something he would regret.

CHAPTER 16

Except for his gray hair, Deb's pop seemed never to age. One might think Jim's constant state of disorientation was a symptom of age, but it was a quality he'd had for as long as Deb could remember.

When Jim/dad traveled, by foot, by car, or by boat in his later years, he turned his head, anxiously checking his orientation. He looked into the distance, halted his progress, and scratched his head.

When they visited Rome, he was so caught up in hunting for something matching the map that he didn't notice when Deb slipped behind him. Instead of being at his side, the unasked-for service she'd always provided, she decided to hang back and just observe as he wandered into the maze of unknown streets. Despite the appearance of being lost, perhaps he knew what he was looking for and could smell it in the wind.

He always used to say to her, trying to start a conversation, "So, have you found the meaning of life?" She thought this was typical of his awkward sense of humor, yet also absorbed it as her mission.

Perhaps I will find the meaning of life and bring it back to Pop. He's been waiting around a long time since the fall.

This waiting around seemed to have something to do with Jim's elf-like non-aging. Falling past brick walls after gravity had pulled him from inside the building, he waited for the accelerated conclusion of his painful life. Instead, time slowed to a non-pace, his vision improved, and his hearing sharpened. He was suspended in a hyper-reality. When he finally hit the ground, it seemed as if part of him was still pre-impact, forever in the air. He was badly hurt, but he would recover. Since Jim could not conclude his story, he was forced to wait for meaning to appear.

Deb was the feet on the ground of her father's unconcluded story. She would aim for the beginning, even just before the beginning, and as the story wriggled away, she might at least get the tail end of it.

Deb's wild boar friend made his home with a few other boars and sows on a small wooded island where they had become isolated long ago. Not that they couldn't swim; they could, but chose not to—except for Deb's boar. He fancied himself a currier. Always curious as a piglet, he had wandered into villages and found some people willing to give him food and admire him. As a young boar, he brought an apple back to the island, swimming with it in his mouth. That trick made him very famous. He decided it was his job to bring things back to the island to share with his fellow boars. He brought sheets back from Alfred and Louise's place, and though they weren't tasty, they were useful: torn into squares, one for each boar. The cloth was used to absorb mud and worn as mud jackets. As he grew bigger, he took on political affairs with the people. He didn't know what he was doing, but he felt he had a knack for it. Making incursions into human society, he tried to give wild hogs a voice in the big picture. Humans seemed adept at big pictures.

It was a fine day for an adventure, the boar thought, smelling flowers on the wind. He swam to the mainland, and trotted his boar path beyond the roads of Middleburg. This summer he had started something new: Deliveries for Hotel Pylons. He was a tough old boar now, not afraid of the other dimensions. It's what wild boars are made for, he told himself, charging into the mists beyond Middleburg, up into the hills. The dark woods with heavy mists offered new things to Jeezum, and he loved novelties. It was what made him a great swimmer and lover of humans, this desire for newness.

Jeezum stopped and trimmed back stems from his trail. Once he established a path, he liked to have "stash areas" carefully hidden. He collected various things of interest in his stashes and did not

let them mix. His pretty rock stash area had no
arrowheads in it, for instance. He was proud of
the few arrowheads he had as they represented
different time periods old and new. Each stash was
a category unto itself. He had a mind for inventory.
He was able to hoard, trade, deliver, and share all at
the same time. It was a long way to the Pylons, and
he had arrived at his traditional resting spot.

Deb was waiting in the forest for the recognition
of eyes, to set fauna apart from flora. Often she did
not see the eyes, but she felt them. The puzzle of
nature seemed to shift, and she would find herself
noticing an animal. She thought of all animals as
her friends, even though she had discovered that
she was a natural hunter: defensive, hyperalert, and
ready to strike. Deb had long ago transmuted these
root qualities, slightly evil qualities, distilled over
ages of incarnations into magic. She transmuted
defensiveness into accepting help, hyperalertness
into calm, and readiness to strike into a long-
observing patience, which included empathy. Her
greatest skill was in finding rather than killing.

She sensed her assignments, or they were
brought to her: find and kill the wild boar for meat
and for peace; find A Crisis Averted so that future
generations might get through this time when
another crisis could not be afforded.

The killing part was repellent to Deb. Nonetheless, she accepted the identity of hunter with her study of the subject and her assignment to kill the pig. Deb liked to study; the topic did not matter; if a call to find something was strong, she could not ignore it.

She had her weapons: a pistol with a silencer and a bow Charles had made for her. Deb did not like loud noises. As if hearing her thoughts, the wheels of fortune dropped the pistol with the silencer at the lost and found at school, and Deb was called to the office to pick it up. It had her initials on it. Deb knew nothing of the gun, but took it and learned to shoot it. She practiced with the bow, too. She had never killed anything. She enjoyed target practice: no moral qualms, just taking aim and letting go. The need for weapons in order to kill a wild animal made it all seem wrong to her. If she were a poisonous snake and could kill the boar in one fatal bite, that would seem more natural—not premeditated, and somehow less morally quarrelsome.

She followed the wild boar up the side of a high hill that became the top of a cliff overlooking the sea. It was almost as if she were simply walking with him, only he was about ten feet ahead of her. The boar felt her presence and ignored her completely. No sign of affection or fear did he betray. They could have been companions exploring on a beautiful day, except for the estrangement that came with Deb's weapons and her new role as hunter. Now there was a widening gulf between them into which the boar might decide to disappear. Deb had seen other wild animals do it. You tracked them, never letting them out of your sight, and then they simply disappeared into their place.

The boar led her to a horrible precipice where she wished he would not go, close to the edge of a cliff. She crawled, hugging the earth at a distance. Jeezum stood at the top of the bluff, looking blissfully at the view: indigo waves roaring, sky almost white, and far-off cliffs made of ancient mud, stacked in layers and topped with bushes, grass, and soft green moss. Clearly, he wanted her to join him, to come and see how glorious the landscape was from on high. It was not a good feeling for Deb to observe him on the edge, so much like Jim/dad at the window of the YMCA. She did not feel the same ease with depth that Jeezum seemed to feel.

She decided to wait until the right moment to strike. Not today. She would keep tracking him, learning everything there was to know, and only when the right moment was given would she draw her bow, or pistol. When the moment of readiness was at hand, she would know.

When she finally had the courage to look out to sea from the grassy cliff top, Jeezum had wandered off into some shrubs. At first, she was aware of him rooting around, and when she thought to check on him, he had slipped invisibly back into the wild.

Maybe I can't see A Crisis Averted because of my assumptions about what kind of story it would be. All I have is myself to work with, the same old habits of rearranging material. What I need is not a blue buffalo or a brown buffalo. I need a buffalo of a color that I can't imagine yet.

If Jim/dad was looking for something, he would simply pick up everything in sight, one thing at a time, look at it and say, "That's not it." Deduction, he called it. Deb didn't have the patience for that. She had a hunger for direct communication with an outside source of alien information.

Then she heard a noise inside her head, the sound of a disk being ejected from a computer. Everything seemed to be spinning, and she was looking for orientation. She felt as if she were the disk being ejected—or was she the computer ejecting the disk? *Wherever my consciousness is, I am that. I could be alive, or not alive. I could be the computer, or the disk. Where can I go to be able to see the story?*

Jackson: the name popped into Deb's thoughts, and she felt a change in her consciousness that allowed her to see Jackson's thoughts from the past. Jackson was the janitor who opened the window that broke Jim/dad's fall. Her hands became big, creased hands, milk chocolate in color on the back and coral pink on the inside. They folded over broom handles easily, and tidied everything as he passed from room to room. The janitor, the only one there at the right time to save her father from his fall. Inadvertently, as if by intuition, he saved a life just by opening a window. Doctors in white coats were respected for saving lives in the time of Jim's suicide attempt, but janitors, especially African-American janitors, went unrecognized.

The air in the conference room felt so heavy that he thought he might suffocate before rotating the crank handle enough times to raise the window, letting some air in. He wouldn't normally open windows so close to the end of his shift, because he'd have to come back and shut them, but he had a nagging feeling that something bad was in the air today. Let it all out, he thought, all that bad feeling. It was a nice day outside and he felt the improvement immediately. Often bad things do reveal themselves when you are taking out the trash, he thought as he pushed the collected garbage down the hall.

It wasn't long after that that the sirens came. He went to close the window because his shift was over, but the window was skewed and wouldn't shut. He looked outside and saw what the trouble was. Directly below the window Jackson had opened, a man was flattened, face down on the pavement. Apparently, he had crashed through from above. As Jackson left the building, he could see the white men's faces looking out from the high-up windows to view the scene: ambulance staff dressed in white, surrounding the body. It was hard to know if the man was alive or dead. He had no shoes, and his feet were red and inflamed. That must be Mr.

Exlander, that odd cat, Jim. Athlete's foot, real bad, poor man. There's not a shoe in Kentucky he can wear in comfort, save the flip-flops required for the showers here at the YMCA. Jackson looked down at his own shoes as he started to walk home. Could be better, could be worse.

Deb opened her eyes and looked at her own shoes. They were falling apart at the seams. She got out a needle and thread and started making repairs, drawing the needle with its thick black thread through the thick red leather where it joined in seams along the side. They were pretty nice shoes, her Mary Jane clogs. Much too nice for the kind of work she was doing, building a house, and being a beekeeper. But they slipped on so easily. Enjoying life was what she felt cut out for, as if there were no concern about survival. *Trying so hard to stay alive sucked the fun out of it.* Hard labor does not express who I am, she thought. The music of life seemed frenzied, but she heard a calm and pleasant melody within it, and wanted only that. *The frenzy is not even music; just an annoying command to keep moving.*

The window broke Jim's fall, and saved his life. Deb hated to think of that first impact with the window, and how the metal must have broken his back. Could it have been a wooden window? Somehow, she never imagined that it was. Recovery was a miracle. Death chewed on Jim until finally he fell out of death's mouth. After nursing his wounds and resting, he lived again.

Jim's crisis was vocational . . . Skyscrapers tempt suicide . . . Don't change anything in your life because you think it will help the outcome of events . . . It doesn't matter what happens, what matters is your life . . . Evasive wisdom swirled around in Deb's head. She remembered how Jim/dad used to pretend to be a tree for her, and she would climb up into his branches. He stood with his knees bent, legs apart, arms raised, and elbows bent, giving her the maximum amount of places to scale and hold onto. Since he was a tree, he didn't help her. He stood sturdily in position while she hung from his arm, until she reached his chest, and then he held her in his arms, the tree of life.

CHAPTER 17

Louisa and Alfred waited. They waited for the baby to come, they waited for the end of the wild boar's pestilence, and they waited wishfully for meat. Everything was wishful, nothing certain. They lived under the rule of contradictory feelings. The house felt stale and confining, yet they were reluctant to leave it. They needed the confines of their known world. They clung to each other and at the same time couldn't stand the nearness of each other. These feelings convulsed in the air around them, with short breaks of blissful rest. Like wandering magnets, they encountered each other in the house, instantly repelling or attracting, depending on some unknown force that turned them this way and that.

Louisa thought about her unborn baby in the twilight hours most of all. She thought about the baby when she sang softly in her quiet room. She liked to sing every day as a sort of sound meditation. Strange voices had been coming to her lately, a different language. *Monken sprawn the tallerhoost . . .* She sang whole made-up operas of nonsense words. Where did they come from? She suspected the strange words were coming from the baby growing inside her. She hoped it was a baby. She had never had a baby before, she had no pregnant peers, and it was hard to believe that something so wonderfully normal could happen.

It didn't seem too far-out to suppose that she could be carrying an alien creature. She often felt paranoid about the whole thing. What was becoming of her? Her breasts were like overgrown sea creatures, striped red with expansion lines, huge areolae like the heads of jellyfish dancing in the deep blue depths; and below, her belly swelled like a fertility goddess's.

Alfred had more in common with their dog, Francesca. Both were devoted to the metamorphosis at their periphery, Louisa. Alfred had committed to whatever happened at this point. He gave up his options, and took the grab bag of the undisclosed. How had it happened that a man like himself who must know everything before he started, a man who did not take risks with people of unknown characteristics, surrendered to a woman whose merits were in constant flux, so slippery and evasive that she escaped comparison?

It might have happened in imitation of the dog. Not knowing what else to do, Alfred took his lead from the dog, who did his job by lying down in a watchful place, at rest yet alert, not doing anything unless asked. Sometimes Francesca would be Louisa's messenger to Alfred, like the head servant telling him what the mistress wanted. His duty to Louisa eclipsed all other values. This was something he could only understand through Francesca's example. *Thank God for the dog lighting my way.*

Alfred had been through many indignities that he tried to take with dignity, the serial collapsing of parts of his life along with all life. Shifting geography ripped his political reputation to pieces. He'd put the pieces back together so many times, he'd begun to wonder . . . Francesca was lying by the door all white and fluffy, her kindly bulk protecting their home. As if aware of his thoughts, she gave him a concerned look. Turning to her, he asked, "How deep is this shit?"

Not being able to provide meat for Louisa in her time of need was a last straw. But there had been many last straws. He thought he would have left her long ago. Women always made him feel horrible about himself. It took about four months with a woman before a feeling of worthlessness sank in, and he ached for an old familiar routine of drinking too much. He made excuses. He pretended to be the one who needed to cut loose. Louisa was a terrible, aggressive woman. Of course, she was extremely nice, too. When she smiled, she all but forced you to smile back.

Francesca answered him belatedly with a question, "If fear is in your heart, what else might be there?" Messages from the dog came not in spoken words; they came like an orb of warmth, traveling with intention from her dog body. The orb came close, touched and melted him so that he could hear the words come through his heart and into his head.

He still had connections in Avignon, France. An odd sort of trade was all it amounted to. He sent his old friend Pierre paperbacks and other antiques he bought from the Lecturing Ladies, and Pierre sent him official governmental stationery, signature stamps, and documents pilfered from the drawers of his old workplace, as well as French business clothes.

The dead, people still in half-life, were able to make boats out of weeds and travel the seas. Not everyone knew this was possible. Few talked with the dead about their interests, and few believed them since they were only half there. But Alfred always felt the power of his forebears, sometimes unpleasantly but mostly with sincere pride. It was not hard for him to believe that the dead influenced our everyday lives. Jim was making many overseas deliveries back and forth between Avignon and Middleburg. People, Alfred believed, still needed their illusions; at least he did. He needed to believe he was somebody important. So he kept the trade going.

The presence of something foreign had a certain authority. He tried to preserve his strangeness in this small town that became too familiar too fast. It was the language school that had brought him here originally, to talk French politics with the students and give them a taste of French life. He was supposed to go to Washington, D.C. to talk about terroir, or "the taste of place" and to deliver a message to the then president, Ms. Attica Outwater: the French were closing their borders to American fast food, period. The Great Wobble came and he never left Middleburg, pretty sure that D.C. no longer existed. He never heard from a governmental agency again. He himself was the only semblance of a governmental agency, having scavenged his props from his old defunct job in Avignon, head culinary defender at Food Quality International, or FQI. Perhaps he was really an actor interpreting a runaway script.

All their furniture had been brought over from France. The couch he was sitting on had been in the FQI library. It was upholstered with a grapevine pattern, and had throw pillows in the shapes of cheese, bread, and bacon. He threw Francesca a bacon pillow, and she hid it under the couch. Yes, the bacon and the cheese were maddening. They had to go. He threw her the rest of the bacon and the cheese as well. "We have to get real bacon, Francesca. Before Louisa kills us both." Francesca began licking her paw, the one she had hurt in a scuffle with the wild boar.

She had used her dog dish to lure it into the house as a possible food source. It came in through her dog door; she was a large dog. The wild boar, once tricked into coming inside, panicked, charged straight for the bedroom, pulled the sheets off the bed, then tore at a box of papers underneath the bed as if it was just the meal it had been searching for. Francesca was used to dealing with people. She had been trained at Dog Diplomacy International, or DDI. When she put up her paw in the "stop" gesture, the boar seemed to think she was offering it for a taste and gently nibbled the paw, drawing a bit of blood. Francesca, horrified, went to get Louisa from the singing room, normally off-limits. Louisa with her soft, magical voice was able to sing the boar out of the house. "Sing away all your obstacles," Louisa would say. But Francesca was not bred for singing. She came from a long line of non-howling dogs.

Afterward, Louisa lay down on the mud-stained bed and slept in the mess. When Alfred came home, she told him a dream about wild boar barbecue. Full of longing, she was certain it was a prophetic dream. When Francesca showed Alfred her paw and told him her side of the story, he began concocting his plan to pressure the neighbors into killing the wild boar. He could butcher and cook, but he was no hunter. Apparently, neither was his dog.

Louisa came into the room, suspicious of the silence. "What's going on in here? Where is the bacon and cheese?" she demanded.

"I thought it would be better to hide them. They're relics," Alfred said.

"How could you? Murderer! I'll die without bacon and cheese!"

"You've lived this long. If you can hang on a bit longer, perhaps there will be real bacon, not pillow bacon."

"You don't have the guts to kill a wild boar, Alfred, I know it."

"You're right, but the butcher always knows the hunter."

"She'll never do it. She's a story hunter, not an animal killer."

"I'll bring in the French Heritage Defense if she doesn't."

"I'm so bored of war," she sang in a sigh. Even though there had been no wars since the Great Wobble debilitated all military powers, Louisa harbored a great anger over the boredom ceaseless wars had caused her, the drones droning on in their tweed jackets about who killed who. She twirled onto the couch, landing on her back with her knees bent over his legs in mock violent exhaustion. "Tell me a story," she said.

Alfred rested his hands on her knees, covered in brown leggings. He looked straight ahead, concentrating. "This is the story I've been told about my ancestors who left France and went to America. They did not fall into any of the worrisome categories of history. They had a sugar plantation in the South, but not in the time of slavery. They left France as Jews, but not fleeing any war. They only came to America looking for jobs and someone to marry. They came to New Orleans so they wouldn't have to learn any English. They sold rags and scrap metal at first, traveling door to door. They worked hard and dreamed big. One of them on his rag and scrap metal selling routes said upon visiting a fine plantation, 'Reserve this place for me.' That became the family plantation, ever after called Reserve. That family in New Orleans eventually employed whole towns, either in their clothing stores or on the sugar plantation."

Louisa's big white belly, covered in a long T-shirt, popped out from her thin form. He took a deep breath, suddenly aware they were both relaxing; bored into a semiconscious state. He stroked her legs and watched her belly move slightly. She was awake but in a soft, focused stillness, feeling the subtle movements inside her belly. Maybe a tiny arm or leg was adjusting itself within the womb. Francesca slept at his feet. Alfred felt the awareness all around them, the air thick with it, like a drug or a lucid dream. His eyelids wetly clung as they closed on something, some lifesaving grip to another heartbeat.

Dr. Rosemary would be arriving soon. Louisa always tried to look her best for the midwife—she wasn't really a doctor, though Alfred called her one. Louisa suspected he felt uncomfortable with any word that had the word "wife" as part of it. He, as dutiful as he was, needed the illusion of freedom. Louisa stood at the mirror, rubbing half a beet on her cheeks and lips. She unbraided her hair and fluffed it around her face, trying to mitigate the look of her pale swollen skin and her tired expression. She practiced her smile and oiled her teeth to make it bigger and brighter. She didn't want the midwife to say anything depressing again, like if she couldn't get meat, she had better eat insects—for protein.

Alfred was in his study, counting his shipments: the antiques to be sent to Pierre and the items he expected in return. It was busywork, something to do until Dr. Rosemary arrived. His wife was not well, though she tried to hide it. Sometimes he thought she did not look like she had the strength to bear a child.

Wife: the word came to him lately though they weren't married. He told Louisa he would never marry; he didn't know why he was still with her. They had a fight once. He had planned to end it that day, early in their relationship, before things went too far, but something happened. He couldn't remember and he hadn't made his exit and so it went too far. And he was never able to bring it up again. He just went along. He went so long that when he heard the word wife he thought of her. He was careful never to say the word out loud.

Finally, Louisa came in and sat in the rocker in a corner of his study. She was the most beautiful woman he had ever seen. Her curves stretched into a dream. Like rare flowers, her eyes were designed to attract many visitors. Variegated blue-green irises, dotted black in the middle, opened like morning glories on a white sky. Animal-like, her lashes stuck out in spikes to protect her perceptive oasis, her brows further emphasizing that her views were her own. Her belly added one more unbelievable curve, something both obvious and hidden under her long, thin shirt-dress. She looked better, not as pale as she had been. Dr. Rosemary had said she was anemic, and warned that pregnant women needed more of all sorts of nutrients found in meat. Alfred didn't know how he was supposed to get meat. In France, wild boar had been popular for hams, bacon, chops, roasts, and pâté. The wild boar was the only edible animal that Alfred had seen in years.

Finally, Louisa spoke, tears streaking down her face as if they had been welling up a long time.

"I'm not going to eat insects," she said. "I don't care what the midwife says."

"What are you talking about? Of course you won't eat insects—what did Dr. Rosemary say?"

"Last time, she said that I was anemic and if I didn't get meat to eat, then I'd better eat insects or else the baby might not come out right, that's what she said." Louisa pushed the last words out in a tearful shout. She stomped from the rocker to the bedroom, where she heaped a puffy blanket on herself and peeked at the clock. "Ten minutes till she gets here," she muttered.

Alfred was sitting on the edge of the bed, his hand on her back, or what he supposed was her back, under the mound of blue comforter.

"She's never on time," he said. "Our baby will be the first thing to be on time in thirty years. We have time, Louisa, to make this right. I'll get you meat very soon. I'm sure the wild boar has come to us for that reason." He continued stroking her back lightly, saying, "You won't have to eat insects. They would only make you barf, and we have had enough barfing!" He peeked under the blanket to see her face. The word "barf" made her smile a little. The red on her cheeks was smeared now, and he saw it wasn't real. She was as pale as ever except for her red eyes and nose, but he pretended not to notice. He realized that the doctor was of no help. They had to do everything themselves, just the two of them. "Rosemary is a worrywart," he concluded.

An urgent bark came from the front door: Francesca warning them of the doctor's arrival. "I'll get it," Alfred said.

Tiny Dr. Rosemary was there on the stoop, with a heap of stinging nettles poking out of her basket. Her dirty blond hair was absolutely straight and cut in a boyish style like a pixie. Almost before Alfred had stepped back, she zoomed to the kitchen table and put down her latest prescriptions with the force of someone who knows she is right.

Always she came with something for Louisa to eat, usually something Louisa could barely stand. The first trimester, it had been sprouts: bean sprouts, alfalfa sprouts, sunflower sprouts, or just about any sort of seed Dr. Rosemary found to sprout. Louisa chewed them joylessly, for the baby's sake. Last time, she brought crickets in little cages. Louisa set them free and hid the cages. She had not told Alfred about the insect prescription until today. Louisa felt the midwife just did not understand her repulsion for eating insects like a fish eating bait off a hook.

"It's all about protein now," Dr. Rosemary was saying again. "You're building another body. It takes meat to make meat. You look terrible, like I could blow you over with one breath."

Dr. Rosemary reached out and pushed a palm against Louisa's shoulder, testing the strength of her resistance. Louisa braced herself. Her dislike of the midwife grew as her time came closer. She stared over Dr. Rosemary's shoulder, steadying her inner gaze on the image of the wild boar, her anger resting calmly there, giving her strength.

"Not bad. You're stronger than you look. But remember, we're in the last innings here. This is the time to gain weight and store energy. At the very least, don't wash the herbs. You may get some protein that way."

"OK, no washing, then. I'll just steam them and eat them with every meal," Louisa said, pretending to go along. In truth, her outburst with Alfred had cinched her detachment, and her faith. She had had enough. She'd tried all these months to be good, and to hell with it. She wasn't going to get all wrapped up in the dos and don'ts of pregnancy anymore, not when it felt wrong to her. *I'll do it my way and it's going to be OK. Alfred promised to get meat for me. The midwife only makes me barf with her sprouts and crickets. Alfred says I'm beautiful, while the midwife said I looked terrible. I am secretly firing her.* She couldn't openly dismiss Dr. Rosemary because the little woman's knowledge and healing were legendary, and the community would be outraged if they felt she wasn't handling the pregnancy right. Louisa believed the wrong way was sometimes the only way to go forward, that forward motion would eventually lead to the one big destination, the eventuality of everything. Yet forward motion was not inevitable. It was possible to elude every eventuality for eternity, it seemed.

As she did the morning chores, Deb found herself thinking of Miranda, feeling her come near like a nudge in the air around her head, that psychic sense a mother sometimes had of her child's movements. She had just planted a little tree that had grown too big for the pot she had put the seed in many years ago. It was sort of a family tree. That had been the intention, but it seemed funny to plant a specific family tree when there were so many trees exactly like this one growing all around, and they put off deciding where to plant it. Until this morning, when Deb realized it was too big for the pot, and there was a hole over yonder where it would be easy to plant. For such a dirty job, Deb wore a pair of soccer shoes, black with white stripes. They had been Miranda's, who had briefly played soccer and then grew out of the shoes and lost interest in the sport. Deb found them quite comfortable, and had pretty much ruined them with overuse. Miranda wore pretty shoes now. She was always on the lookout for flats with interesting texture and style. *My baby has always been such a princess.*

As if called by the thought, Miranda walked down Ruth's Road into the clearing where Deb and Charles were building the house. Over the summer, the house started to take form. It was more than just a plan and foundation for a house: it was a home in the making.

Deb was pumping water at the well when she saw Miranda in a flowing yellow sundress with buttons and a belt. As was their custom, they ran to each other, arms out like long-separated lovers.

"Mommy!" Miranda shouted.

"Baby!" Deb shouted back as they met, hugging and grinning. "I missed you, you look a little sunburned, are you OK? How was the Grand Canyon?"

Miranda was glowing, her dark curls tied back with just a few stragglers framing her face here and there, her eyes bright and clear in their arched hollows. Seeing her was like discovering a ripe red tomato in her garden, pride and hope about the not-so-distant future mixed into great joy.

"It was awesome—you went there, didn't you, when you were a kid?" Miranda asked.

"Yes, but there was no Mississippi Sea to cross, and it was a real tourist attraction back then. There were Japanese people taking pictures and French people in short shorts with hairy armpits. We didn't enjoy the place all to ourselves the way you must have—did you see any people?" Deb asked.

"Come on, I'll help you get the water."

"Can you climb the hill in those shoes?"

Miranda's shoes looked like something Cleopatra would wear if she had to play Jesus in a theater production: thin cords of leather tracing designer hieroglyphs from toe to ankle. *How does she manage to be such a princess in these times of bare bones?*

Miranda looked into her mother's face and smoothed back a wild wave of Deb's hair. "You look so . . ." Miranda hesitated. "So old," she finished.

"Oh well," Deb said.

"No, it's not bad. You look like you're old enough to be my mother."

Deb let it lie. This was no time to be vain; there were more important things, like measuring up to your child's expectations. Deb had looked too young to be a mother, and now, finally, it was believable that she was old enough to be a proper mother. So fine, let the healing begin.

Miranda pumped the metal lever up and down, filling the bucket that hung from the spout.

"I don't know how you do this every day," Miranda said.

Deb flexed her arm and showed Miranda her muscle. They both broke down laughing. "It's the biggest thing on you!" Miranda said.

While Deb appeared older, Miranda returned ten years younger than when she left, it seemed.

"I have something to tell you, Mom," Miranda said as she carried the water, one bucket in each hand, back to hangar B1.

"We could make a place for you here," Deb said, "or if we get the house done soon, you and Ramey could stay there. Your dad and I don't mind living in the hangar. We're used to it."

"Mom, I will. I don't know where else to go. I'm pregnant and Ramey isn't with me, I don't know what happened."

"Is he OK? Did you two have a fight?" Deb asked.

"I think he got sucked into the vastness. Maybe he went crazy, I'm not sure. It's like he couldn't stop. We got to a desert and he just kept saying 'one last dune' and then would fall apart, laughing over some creature he had found that I couldn't even see. Half the time, I felt like he wasn't there, not on the same plane as I was. It's like we entered a landscape that was a bad drug for him. He promised he would come back to Middleburg when he completed his journey. I couldn't go with him. It was heartbreaking, but I had to do it for myself—and the baby," she said, looking down at what Deb could now see was a little extra roundness in her belly.

Miranda suddenly started crying, and could no longer talk in an understandable key. It was an unbelievable nightmare to hear her daughter in such pain and hopelessness, and there was nothing she could do to stop it.

"How do you know you're pregnant?" Deb softly ventured.

It was not the first time Miranda had been pregnant, but time never seemed to go in a forward motion long enough for Miranda's pregnancies to come to term. Deb wondered if it was the same baby who tried to come before.

Miranda seemed to calm down. It was easier for her to talk about her pregnancy than to think about Ramey, though the two were linked.

"I know. It's the same as before, exactly as before, all the feelings, even my thoughts. It's like I'm back in that time when it was possible for me to bring that life, the same one who almost came before," Miranda said.

"It'll be good to stay put here for a while, focus on the time being. I think if you pay close attention to the present moment, maybe the pregnancy will continue and develop normally," Deb said.

"That's what I think, that's why I came home. Ramey must hate me for abandoning him. We had fun for the first week, then I don't know what happened."

"You're tired. Lie in my bed while I set up an area for you."

"OK."

Miranda slept for two days, sleeping off sadness, unspeakable sadness.

When she recovered, Deb said, "Maybe it's time to open your late birthday present . . ."

The idea of a box wrapped up made Miranda glad, just what she had dreamed of: a white box with some unknown inside. The tradition of birthday presents was as sweet as ever to her. The present was not in a box, though. Deb brought her attention to something hidden under a sheet by the wall, and Charles unveiled the present that he and Deb had been collaborating on while she slept. It was the very blender that had been part of her childhood, in a time when every normal household had electricity. It was a strange, fond memory of the past, and just to have some connection to her former life was a comfort. They had adapted the blender to current times. It was hooked up to a stationary bicycle to become a human-powered blender.

"Let's concoct a breakfast drink," Deb said.

Miranda loved it, the old blender restored to its former purpose. There were so many things she used to make that required a blender: dressings, dips, smoothies, and purees. She enjoyed cooking from the time she had been allowed to help her mother with meals. It was an art form that allowed her to receive a sort of fame that was more like love. It was never hard to find fans when you could transform food into a memorable shared experience.

No one mentioned her age this birthday because no one wanted to disrupt the reality of time that her pregnancy inhabited. Ten years forward or back might not make much difference to most people, but to a fetus it could be fatal.

"Mom?" Miranda said, looking up from her drink, tears beginning to well.

"It's OK, you don't have to talk about it right now," Deb said.

"I wish we had gone to the Grand Canyon together when I was younger."

"Do you remember when we saw sea horses, jellyfish, and the walrus at the Coney Island aquarium when you were young?"

"Of course I do! If it wasn't for that, I don't think I'd have any faith at all. Did you know sea horses mate for life? I wish you and Dad hadn't waited so long to live together as a couple. We could have been a family."

"I thought you were too young to be nostalgic for that nuclear family part of the American dream." Deb laughed uneasily.

"Maybe it's her influence," Miranda said, giving a nod toward her belly.

"We are family. We're just a funny family, a running-late family."

"I love your guts, Momma."

Charles installed himself in the loft, giving

Deb and Miranda some privacy. Miranda still wasn't used to having her mother and father in the same house. She grew up with separate realities, her mother-world and her father-world. Charles listened from above to the different sort of closeness Miranda had with her mother. He felt jealous of Deb and sympathetic toward Miranda. Why had they waited so long? It hadn't been his choice. A nice, normal family would have been fine with him. Deb wasn't a nice and normal woman, though. He wasn't exactly angry about it. She fascinated him. But it was satisfying somehow to hear Miranda voice her regrets. He too missed that something that had never been, the part where he would have been with them when they saw the sea horses, part of all those childhood memories, the outings with Mom and Dad.

"Thanks. I love you, too," Deb said.

CHAPTER 18

It wasn't long before Miranda made herself at home and found ways to spend her time contentedly while the baby grew inside her. She regarded it as a happy convalescence. Meanwhile, Deb was getting restless. Satisfied that Miranda was doing OK, she wanted to get back to her mission of finding A Crisis Averted.

Louisa came over almost daily, having found one other person in her predicament to talk with about food. Miranda and Louisa had both become obsessed with the idea of meat. Miranda cooked all sorts of things for Louisa. With Miranda's culinary genius, offerings of ingredients came out of the woodwork, and often they had guests for dinner. Every now and then, Alfred would come over, too, always asking, "Have you killed the boar yet?" Charles promised Deb would take care of it, corroborating Alfred's assumption that the boar was under Deb's authority.

Pursuing A Crisis Averted seemed to have led her to the boar. *Will pursuing the boar lead me to the story?* Deb had been mostly vegetarian long before this new age of scarcity and renunciation. Yet in truth, she was not as vegetarian as she looked. She remembered fondly the bonding smell of cooking meat, how people gravitated toward the smell and shared the welcome bounty. Then people became too snooty to eat just anything that smelled good. The shift in consciousness seemed to come with the shift in the earth's deep tectonic plates.

Something was changing again. Alfred had become annoyed enough to place the ultimatum of war on the boar's head. Louisa and Miranda were pregnant enough to demand whatever food they wanted. Their passions seemed contagious, and the desire for meat was no longer mute and forgotten.

Only queasy Deb, charged with the actual killing, seemed to remember the long Lenten promise to live deeply in peace, and to harm no other being.

And then there was the fact that the wild boar had turned up in the first place. Was that some sort of providence? For what purpose did the boar befriend her?

Deb planned her next hunting expedition to track the boar through the Pylon in the Hills, an alternate reality where Jeezum was rumored to have gone, or maybe returned to. The Pylon in the Hills was said to be a transformative temple created by godlike beings who used abandoned cell phone towers as gateways into a world between our world and the next. The Pylons were a cosmic force stationed right on earth, influencing earthly goings-on without being earthly themselves. Most people avoided the mountain area because they didn't like getting lost, and it was always foggy and rainy up there. It would be a good place to meditate on the story and perhaps kill the boar. At least she could get away from Albert's constant checking in on her progress.

Now that everyone was meat-crazed, they would be happy to see her go, with her gun and bow. *Sometimes you just have to keep going, follow through, and see where things lead.*

She couldn't take much with her because the Pylon spirits demanded pilgrims come like babies, without a thing of their own. She could hide the bow and the gun somewhere before she got too close.

She ate a hearty breakfast before Charles woke, though he did rouse enough to see to it that Deb had her bow and gun and to congratulate her on the meat she would surely bring home. Miranda didn't hear a thing as Deb took the last apple, grabbed a long-sleeved overshirt, slung a canteen of water over her shoulder, and headed for the hills. Not knowing why, Deb turned back to get her manuscript—just the memory card from her Alpha Smart—and stuck that in her back pocket.

She knew the general direction and embarked with nothing more than an apple and water for sustenance. *Perhaps I should have left the apple for Miranda.*

But she was already hungry, or afraid; she couldn't tell which. She took a step closer to the fog with each bite of the apple. She was still a good distance away, a safe distance, but she could see where this was going. Unless she turned back, she would end up walking right into the fog of confusion out of which the towers tapered. Did Jeezum go here? she wondered. At one point, she saw a stretch of tracks, dainty almond impressions side by side in the mud, but then nothing. It was bushy and rocky now that she had reached the highlands. There wasn't soft ground for making hoof tracks.

When Deb reached the fuzzy edge of the Pylon in the Hills, she stopped for a rest. Instead of charging right in, she decided to sleep in a mock grave. She dug out a hollow, covered it with branches, and then lay inside for warmth and meditation to see if anything came from procrastination and self-imposed exile.

These words ached in the earth, rolled up inside it like a newspaper ready to swat a fly. She felt the pull of social obligations against her selfish desire for solitude. *Damn, I have to tell Charles where I am and when I'll be back. He'll wonder when it gets dark. I should have just told him my ideas and my plans . . . I don't know why I can't admit the truth, that I don't want to use a weapon and that Jeezum has entered the Pylons.*

She had been lying there peacefully for half an hour before she realized this. She poured a bowl of water, put her communication stone in, and sent Charles a message about where she was. She hadn't really thought about how long she would stay, so she just said, "For a while." A short time later, the bowl of water lit up with a return message from Charles. "It's supposed to rain tomorrow, so you might want to plan on coming back this evening or early in the morning." She sent a quick message back: "Thanks, maybe so, but no promises."

It was sunny and the pine boughs gave off their fragrance, but a cool breeze came and the sky was changing. She put some of the small, soft boughs under her back so her resting place was more like a chaise lounge from which she could view the forest, and the chasm of mountain and sky.

Yellow leaves were falling down like a sparkly sheer curtain waving through the stillness of trees. Light hit each floating leaf and highlighted movement in fellowship with stillness. *Two chipmunks flitted along a fallen limb, teasing the eye of awareness.* She felt she could stay there a long time, as if her purpose in life was just to commune with nature. *Could it be that simple? This love trumps all competing quests for meaning. Could I tell Jim/dad that the meaning of life is to commune with nature? Is that what happened when Hurricane Betsy healed him? Can the next crisis be averted this way?*

Yet there were other things in life that would bring her down from the mountain of communion. She had to go back to high school, she had to finish

226

the art and science project, she had to decipher sweet cicely, Charles needed her help finishing their beyond-the-American-dream house, and well, who knew what else. The fact was you never knew what your duties were in life. Nothing was set. You just had to be there. You didn't have a calling; instead you were on call. You could be called to do anything at any time.

She felt called at that moment to get up and start walking again, find a different place inside the fog…over there in the tall grass where she could rest some more.

Life was only one side of nature. You could commune with nature when you were dead. What made life different than death was that you might be called upon to act in life. In death you rested, full-time.

The shattering was a deep beauty, an infinite crystal of planes. In fact, we knew little of the activities that might have been possible after death. People died eventually, no matter what. They shattered regardless of whether they did the right or wrong thing. It was a wonderful thing for Deb to climb and not look up or down. When the time comes to panic, I'll panic. You couldn't live in the pre-now. It was a lovely horror to be here alone on the mountain where nothing was happening.

Ah, to be quest-less. She was enjoying her dream escape so much that at first she didn't notice the animals. Two tan cougars, one on each side of her, tapped her hands with their paws. Deb jumped up immediately and began walking with purpose. Her hands were scratched, but the nonconfrontational way was best, and she acted as if this sudden departure had been her own idea.

She didn't look at the cougars or her scratched-up hands. She just walked, as if getting to her destination would solve her problems and the cougars would disappear. They seemed to be driving her toward some unconscious path with tall grass on either side. They padded her and continued swiping at her hands. She saw in her mind a small, unpainted wooden house, filled with peace and safety from wild beasts. The path inside the tall grass took her along the edge of the cliffs. She had no idea she was on the edge of the mountainside as the cougars hurried her along. She felt as if she were one of them. That was why she couldn't look at them. She only looked in the direction they were going, trotting forward as if they hunted the same thing.

It started to rain lightly. The sky turned white with fog, then gray with evening. While the mental image of her destination dulled, the instinct of pursuit intensified. She thought of nothing but slogging forward. She forgot any idea of reward, such as killing the boar, escaping the cougars, or finding her story. Fear disappeared like the apple, now that she was on her feet, trotting down the path with these cougars. It was more a matter of keeping pace.

Whatever happened, she was made for it, apparently. They took her to their cave. Her hands were leathery and the fur on her neck stood up. No wonder she was at home. She was not sure where along the path this happened, but she was a great cat, a majestic hunter. The communication stone was where she had left it in a bowl of water, drinking moonlight and storing cosmic intelligence. The cats shredded her pants into a more stylish fringed skirt. They seemed to have a certain style. There were paintings on the wall of people hunting with cats; clawed sculptures made from scavenged love seats. The cats were very expressive and unconventional in their art.

Exploring the cave, she came to a flap, and pushed through it. On the other side, there was a basement with an elevator. A man—he seemed like the maintenance man or an elevator attendant—welcomed her in.

"Madam, I see you have come through the cat door. That was unnecessary. Are you ready to go up to the main floor?"

He pushed a button and stood aside. The doors opened to reveal a small room.

"Make yourself at home; the elevator is slow. It takes about ten minutes."

The room was quite comfortable, like a tiny parlor for sitting by oneself. The floor was checkered linoleum and the walls papered with a cream-colored velvet pattern. At the midpoint, the walls changed to mirrors, and there was a bench for sitting. Deb was just going with the flow of whatever happened now . . . *It's not up to me what gives pleasure and what gives pain—I only respond to God's will by avoiding pain and seeking pleasure. To maintain good health, I must hear the little voice and please it well* . . . She knew there would be a bathroom upstairs, but the elevator itself was so attractive for peeing. She was alone, and she didn't have to ask anyone anything. Deb backed herself into a corner and pulled up her dress, squatted and peed, shaking her butt vigorously afterward to get the droplets off.

Even as she dashed to the trash can with soggy paper towels, she was treated as a clean woman. Surely the guy downstairs would think she was a very sloppy Madam.

When Deb got to the main floor front desk, she realized she was without her luggage. An image came to mind of a red canvas zip-up roll-along type of suitcase that was hers. The luggage seemed not to matter that much. Nothing was very disturbing to her. It was just the way it was.

Instead of reporting her luggage missing, she asked for a copy of The Rita. The Pylon in the Hills would surely have The Rita, perhaps even the original dream scroll. The Rita was known to link pre-and post-Great Wobble worlds. Deb was no longer on the mountain she knew. Some part of her, known as Madam, understood that this was an alternate reality. She had heard of the Pylon in the Hills, and sensed its presence, but she never really believed it was where a split in evolutionary consciousness allowed for a different world.

Yet here she was, brought in by the cats. The young woman at the desk reached into a drawer and brought out a page of The Rita. Deb hesitated, thinking the woman must have misunderstood.

"It's all you need," the woman said.

Deb took a seat in the lobby and read:

> Rita: I'm glad his parents can bail you out!
>
> May: Well, I mean, they are there, but we don't want to ask.
>
> Rita: Of course! But it's good to have someone you can ask, and who can provide if you have to ask.
>
> May: Right. It's good to know that it's not an issue of survival, so much as one of pride.
>
> Rita: Yes, exactly. It is OK to ask for help, though, you know.
>
> May: Yes, of course.
>
> Rita: I was thinking to myself the other day that as I get older, life might be more difficult for me because I don't like to ask for help, yet I might need it more.
>
> May: Even from Hector? Well, don't hesitate to ask me!
>
> Rita: I should practice asking for

help now.

May: Yes, you should. Just with little things. Hey, it took me a while, too, but what helped were people here constantly offering help, so that having help became more of a norm, and I realized there was no shame in asking. That's a recent development, though. I, like you, don't like asking for help. I am often even insulted when it is offered. Ah, stubborn women . . .

Rita: Yes, well, I was thinking of it during my collage workshop—so many things I have to move around. After class, though, everyone pitched in to help me load up my car with hardly any prompting.

May: Oh, nice! Yeah, people are more willing than you think.

Rita: Yes, I mean, I should get used to asking gently for a little assistance or just taking it when offered. I notice how sometimes I resist even being offered help.

May: Same here, I totally understand . . . You can do it yourself, and how dare they think otherwise!

Rita: Got to get over that and enjoy the camaraderie. I'm learning.

It gave Deb a warm feeling. This was what people loved about The Rita: it found you where you were and offered you real life. Whatever was true for The Rita was always true for you. It was quite likely that Miranda had contributed this and was speaking directly to her. The light of love was unbroken and powerful. Then she turned the paper over and there was more, a seemingly unrelated snippet that eerily reminded her of her own long-ago contributions to The Rita:

> The day was cold, and the sky was bright. While walking across the bridge, I was thinking I was a lucky woman.
>
> I had spent the morning in a coffee shop with my laptop in Carol's quiet basement, attending to the business of selling my house and beeswax candles online. When I finished my coffee, my ticket to the café, it was time to go to work, a short walk to the Children's Center. It was almost noon. I gathered up my black things, mad bomber hat, puffy coat, backpack, and put my laptop back into its black case. As I descended the worn marble steps to the street, the sun-brightened historic town greeted me. Brick-faced shops with wooden signs hanging from iron arms flapped gently in the wind. A familiar giant pencil over Main Street Stationery's door marked the general time I was in, early 2000s. Going to work that day, I thought of my stress-free job, the small space it took up in my

life, and I was feeling happy to have some money this month. It was not a lot, but it was almost completely painless to earn. I was abundantly free to enjoy this day.

When I got to the bridge, a woman passed me from the inside. I hardly noticed her, a woman dressed in brown, carrying a purse. As she passed, a check-shaped piece of paper blew in the wind, caught in currents of the rushing waterfall under the bridge.

The paper drifted in the most entertaining way, stolen by one wind, and caught by another. It didn't fall into the waterfall: the wind currents wouldn't let it. The damp mists churning above the crashing waters didn't break the paper down. The short ribbon of paper was taken higher and higher, this way and that. I had a moment to stop and watch it, to see what happened. Finally, it found at least a temporary home up high in a tree, on a tiny island in the river below the falls. There, tossed in the branches, bent in a "u" shape over a limb, the paper finally stopped.

Could the piece of paper have come from the woman dressed in brown? I know I had no checks to lose, no check-shaped lists of things to do on my person. Perhaps it slipped from her fingers, or the wind snatched it from her purse. She marched on, while I stood there fascinated with the flying paper. In all likelihood, it may be a note of distress from some other world not as pleasant as my own.

Again, Deb felt the pull toward the image of a house, and inside was the old woman. Deb liked and trusted her for some inexplicable reason. Maybe it was the smell of tomatoes stewing, the décor of her home, or the fact that she had traveled with nomads and learned how to heal from them. Deb wanted to ask her if she knew of A Crisis Averted. The sweet cicely reminded her of the old woman. Perhaps she was no longer living, but her memory was called up by the smell of this herb and the sound of its name, like an invitation to cross borders and seek help beyond the world of the living. The image faded, yet the feeling of invitation was strong. The blue light was turning green.

It occurred to Deb that what she needed was a word randomizer. She could take every word in the story she had written so far and randomize the words, so that the natural automatic sense would come forward. One order was hidden within another order, camouflaged. If the words were randomized, then the hidden order would stand out in contrast to the disorder.

Deb doubted that they had a word randomizer here, but this place seemed to have stuff. So she went to the front desk again and asked if they had a word randomizer, and they did. Such a comfortable place it was, with spongy orange chairs. She sank into one, her head deep in the oversized molecule. She stuffed the memory card with her manuscript in the slot under the seat cushion, and fell asleep waiting. When she woke up, she reached into another slot under the seat cushions for what she anticipated would be her randomized manuscript. Instead, she found a packet of letters, "from your ancestors" it said on the envelope. They were in French and Deb couldn't read them. She went to the front desk, and instead of asking for a translator, she asked if the letters might be delivered to Middleburg. The woman at the desk replied, "They were already sent to Middleburg, and were returned by wild boar."

Mention of the wild boar agitated Deb. She didn't understand the Pylon in the Hills's postal system, and she didn't have the patience to hear all about it. The communication stone was calling her; she could feel its pulse in her feet. She had to get back on the earth, out of Hotel Pylon and back onto grass, rock, and soil. Heading out the side door, she took off her shoes as soon as the cement ended and on the ground ahead she felt a pulsing path extending her feet like antennae. It was getting dark fast. Somehow, she had the faith to continue in the dark, just going by the feel of the earth beneath her feet. Eventually, she came to the light of her communication stone in the bowl of water where she had left it, and there was Tim waiting for her.

"You're late for school. Charles sent me to walk with you," Tim said.

"I didn't know you knew Charles," Deb said.

"Charles was my mom's friend. They knew each other in college, acted in some plays together."

"Oh, I didn't know any of that . . . weird."

"It's not weird, it's lucky."

"Why lucky?"

"If Charles hadn't known my mom, I wouldn't be here."

"What!? Is Charles your dad?"

"No. It's more complicated. He got my dad out of jail," Tim answered in one long out-breath.

"Whew! You scared me . . . that seems a whole lot less complicated to me," Deb said.

"Everything is complicated to someone. Did you get the boar?"

"No, but I saw him."

"Do you see him now?"

As soon as he asked, Deb felt a connection and locked her eyes on Jeezum's eyes, his camouflaged face melding into the shapes and shadows of the forest. "Yes, he's right there!"

Deb pointed with her finger to the area where the boar stood, and a tree crashed as if marking the spot for Tim to see.

"Wow, you're pretty good with that finger, but I think you're going to need your gun. Here, you left it at the edge of the fog," Tim said, and handed her the gun.

The pig was too astonished to run when the rotten birch limbs fell around him. He seemed intrigued with the new forage available, things on the ground he might normally never see: a nest with a crushed egg, the white birch limb lines randomly slicing the dark forest floor.

The time was right. It was time to do what she had to do. The boar was held captivated by the new white lines of birch, crossed in a crumble around him. Tim was here, encouraging her. The boar was giving her a side view of his body, less than twenty feet away. She had a good shot. There was no better time than now to take his life with as little pain as possible. She took the gun and her aim, an aim she had been practicing from her heart and with her hands, then squeezed the trigger.

Jeezum didn't make a sound but he bolted, and Deb, not wanting to lose him, bolted off after him. Not two minutes later, "He's over here!" Tim shouted. The boar circled back closer to where the shot was taken. Tim, a little afraid, stood off waving so Deb could see where they were. A strange mix of feelings came over her when she got there. Relieved at first, she felt a terrible glee over the kill, and wore a victorious smile. Then when she knelt to inspect the wound, she saw it looked like a perfect heart wound, and she felt a terrible sadness. She started crying. She touched him as he was dying, and felt the last puff of his self vanish into thin air. In that last moment, she felt as if he knew that she was grieving him, and he was looking back on her with compassion and love, just inches above his body. She saw his spiritless form.

She now understood that she had lost her friend the boar, but not her friendship with the boar. The special bond they had and the time they enjoyed together were hers forever, but Jeezum was gone. Then a strange feeling of peace and gratitude, as if this had been the perfect way to say good-bye, just to hold Jeezum this way and feel the last of his life depart, to breathe the last out-breath with him. She whispered into his fur, "Good-bye, Jeezum, enjoy Summerland." She had seen a glimpse in her mind of the place his spirit was going as she held him during those last breaths, and the word Summerland came to her, green fields filled with dandelions. Even so, coming to terms with it and feeling his death was OK, perhaps the way it was meant to be, did not erase her sadness. Her relationship with the boar, her time with him, was a gift. The gift of love comes with sadness we never want to erase, a sweet sadness. *So that's what a friend is.*

"Yes, he's dead," she said, standing up, grief-stricken.

"Are you ready to move on with the process?" Tim asked.

"Yes, I know we can't wait around. I don't want to waste his life."

"OK. Let's go get Alfred."

"Why? I don't even know Alfred," Deb said,

distracted with her boar thoughts.

"You do, too. Anyway, he's our butcher," Tim said.

"Really? He can do that? I thought I was going to have to do it." Deb was starting to feel eager, now that her tears were under control, to get organized and start taking care of the death details.

"I've seen him through the window, doing butcher performances for his wife. Looks like he knows what he's doing," Tim said.

"Oh, that's right, me too, I don't know why I didn't think of that. I'm so glad, actually. I'd rather have it professionally done, I don't want to waste or misuse any of him. I want to incorporate all of Jeezum into our lives," Deb said.

∘⟶ CHAPTER 19 ⟶∘

Alfred was often at home, with the flag of France planted near. Tim looked in the window and waved, then went to the door and knocked. Instead of following, Deb waited at the mailbox. She didn't want to look at anyone. She was still feeling complicatedly sad.

"Deb!" Alfred called out, waving her over.

She was ushered into the living room, where Tim, Louisa, and Francesca were already gathered. Looking down, she said, "Well, it's done."

"Tim told me how you almost killed him without even a weapon. I commend you," Alfred said.

Deb hadn't had time to process it all. She wasn't sure she wanted to take credit, but that seemed like the easiest thing to do. She remembered the boar's lifeless body and held back a wave of tears.

"Are you a real butcher? Can you take care of the butchering details? I don't feel up to it, but I'd like the boar to be fully utilized in our lives, back into our community," Deb said.

"Shhhh!" Louisa said in a mock whisper. "He's

supposed to be an important political figure!"

"I don't care anymore. Perhaps the butcher is an important political figure in these times. I'm happy to do it. It's what I've been hoping for. The process of transforming a killed animal into meat, cutting it into usable parts with a purpose, is the path to peace with our needs," Alfred said.

Louisa threw her arm around his shoulder. "Attaboy!" she said, and waddled upstairs.

"Where are you going?" Alfred asked.

"To get dressed for the outing," she shouted from upstairs, rooting through Alfred's wardrobe, looking for a flannel shirt that would button over her belly.

"She killed him magically, almost by accident, except the tree was rotten and more amusing to the pig than deadly. Good thing I brought the gun. She had a perfect shot and she took it. The boar fell just inside the edge of the fog, in the direction of the Pylons. Take the route straight up from Deb's place. You'll see an apple core in the path. Keep going. I've marked the rest of the way with white cloth ties on branches," Tim said.

"That's often the way it happens. The best hunters don't try too hard. I'll bring the boar back here on a sled, but I don't think Francesca can be trusted in situations with raw meat . . . and since it looks like Louisa is coming along—can you dog-sit for a while?" Alfred asked Tim and Deb.

"Of course," Tim said.

Deb looked at the dog and the dog looked at her. "Sure," she confirmed. Perhaps mundane duties would ease her grief and give her space to be with what happened. It seemed no one understood her loss. No one else had been drawn to the boar, or been friends with him the way she had. Jeezum shared the forest with her as no one else had. His exuberant pig nature, his pigheadedness was a wonderful thing, and she admired his wild boarness. Tim had seen her cry, but even he did not seem to understand. She didn't really want a hug; if she could move through this without attracting attention to herself, so much the better.

Alfred sat at his secretary and pulled out a piece of official French governmental business stationery; then with a very fancy pen, he set down his words in ink: ". . . the great contribution these young"— and he looked at Deb and amended, "students of all ages must make in order to pay back France for the deep sacrifices she has made . . . we appreciate your flexibility in allowing Francesca, official dog representative of France, to come to school today with Deb and Tim." Alfred signed with a flourish.

The air seemed stale and still. Deb was glad to leave but glad also that she had finally been inside their house. She was starting to get used to Alfred and Louisa.

"Going back to school after a vacation is not easy," Deb said as they walked out the door with Francesca.

"Where did you get the idea that we were on vacation?" Tim wanted to know.

"I heard it on the radio."

"I don't know what channel you were on, but our school is not on vacation. The project is due, and we still have some kinks to work out."

"Like what?"

"Well, my brother and father haven't done any work at all, and if they fail, I fail. So we have to get them involved."

"Maybe the dog will help," Deb said.

"Of course. Dogs always help," Tim said.

Francesca seemed to be listening, affirming her role as the interspecies instigator of cooperation.

"Well, tell me, how did Charles get your dad out of jail? And why was your dad in jail in the first place?" Deb asked.

"Long story, it all happened before I was born. My dad only told me about it the other day. He told me he just walked in, and couldn't get back out."

"Why did he walk in, and why couldn't he just walk out?"

"I imagine he was just showing off. He never shows off now because, like, he's learned his lesson, but apparently, one of the things my mom liked about him was his magic tricks. He thought he had perfected the walking-through-walls trick, but found that the reality behind prison walls was harder to walk out of than the reality in front of prison walls. He cockily walked in, but couldn't walk out."

"How does Charles come in?"

"OK, so Charles, as you know, has many practical skills. One of them is masonry. At that time, his walls were in demand as the world was fragmenting. He offered to build some walls inside the prison, and since he offered to do this for free, no one questioned him. He took the wall closest to the barbershop, just across the street from the prison, and built a series of walls in front of it. In each wall, he built a doorway. So, there were three walls with doorways built right in front of the outer wall. Beautiful."

"And so how did that help your dad?" Deb asked.

"We don't know exactly, but it's like the openings in the three previous walls prepared my dad to walk through the fourth wall. As soon as he was out, he went across the street, and the barber fixed him right up as a new and free man. You know, the number three is magic. If you can do something three times, you are the master of it. It doesn't work for everyone, but it sure worked for my dad. Because of that, my mom and dad got back together and I was born," Tim said.

"Funny, I've been wanting Charles to build a wall around our space, but he said he doesn't like to work with stone."

"I've been wanting my dad to do magic, but he says he's afraid."

Everyone left class at 2:30 except for Deb, who

was sleeping on the couch, and Francesca, who sat nearby, guarding Deb's sleep. Francesca believed she had a message for Deb from her mistress. She put her paw up on Deb's arm to check, and sure enough, the vibe was there, so she lay down for a snooze and delivered it by dream mail:

> Hi, it's Louisa. Everyone needs a confidant, and I know you will not judge me. You would be fascinated to know what I have done. I have tried to get your attention, but you seem afraid of me. I heard you are looking for a story about a crisis averted—that's what I did, that's why Alfred and I are still together today.

Deb opened one eye and looked at Francesca, and Francesca opened one eye and looked at Deb. Sensing that the message was not over, both closed their eyes again, the dream still within reach. This time, images and narration came willy-nilly.

First came the image of Alfred, sitting there in that horrible male reluctance, refusing to ripen into lasting love. Arms folded, feet stuck out, exasperated expression on his face, as if to say, "None of this is my fault, I'm not the crazy one." Signaling by his posture that he was sick of it, he wouldn't talk about it, and he was completely incapable of carrying on with a woman once marriage entered her mind. No matter what position he took, he looked immobile.

His attitude transformed his normal good looks, rendering him unattractive. He was sitting there in Louisa's house, her claim in Middleburg; she had sung for a lot more than her supper to "buy" it. It was fall, and he sat in her most comfortable chair near the warmth of her woodstove, rudely taking up space. She went to the bedroom and got his pillow, the one he brought from his bed to hers for his comfort. She shoved it at him. "Take this with you," she said. To her disgust, he took the blue puff with relief and resignation as he walked out the door.

Louisa thought how silly this whole argument was. They had been getting along splendidly, and she wished she had never brought up the idea of marriage. She knew if he left now, it was over. "What about your toothbrush?" she asked, and she stepped aside, indicating he should reenter to retrieve it. As soon as his back was turned, she grabbed a two-by-four that had been lying around. She raised the board high and bonked him on the head, not too hard and not too soft. He was stunned; for a few moments, he just lay there, knocked out. When he came to, he didn't remember the fight, and Louisa never mentioned marriage again. They got along splendidly once more.

When Louisa first met Alfred, she told him she never wanted to marry; she wasn't even sure about monogamy. Perhaps that was why he seemed so depleted when she wrote a poem about marriage for him. She didn't know she would have a change of heart. In any case, she never mentioned marriage again, even after she got pregnant. Without the slightest intention of being anything other than single, he slipped into the role of husband. It was a blind spot. Most people thought of him as Louisa's husband and didn't even know Louisa's name, simply calling her Alfred's wife. It had been like this for seven years.

Was this a crisis averted? Was this living happily ever after? This, Louisa would say, was tolerance. It was like when the one you loved had a hole in their consciousness, and all you could do was love them anyway.

Deb opened one eye. Francesca wagged herself awake and got up, affirming that the story had come to an end, giving little pounces of readiness to go for a walk. Deb sat up and rubbed her eyes. Louisa was proud of this? Deb felt a little ashamed to have even heard of this violent and deceitful resolution to a lovers' quarrel. Yet Louisa thought she would be fascinated, as if Deb was a connoisseur of unsavory power plays. It brought on a shocking and dreadful feeling in Deb, as if she had discovered a wound and felt guilt by proximity.

CHAPTER 20

In 2009, Charles had bought a formidable quantity of sea salt, enough to last for decades, and boxes of seaweed to eat when the ocean turned black with oil, death, and radiation. It seemed a little overly pessimistic at the time, but it had come in handy over the years and especially now, when there was meat to be salted and put by, bacon to be made. Charles did not always relish being right about the state of the world, but this time his forethought had saved the day, and everyone knew it. "Hope for the best and prepare for the worst" had been his motto. His mantra these days was "That's just the way it is." It was a contagious coping strategy. Everyone said it now, like old-fashioned coins of wisdom being passed around.

Today, Charles was feeling highly optimistic. "A swarm in June is worth a silver spoon," he found himself chanting at odd times under his breath. There were still two weeks left in June. They caught one swarm; perhaps there would be another. After Deb killed the boar, everyone seemed to have a mission to participate in community life. It was like helium in his heart; it was what he liked about the bees. They put the well-being of the hive above their individual needs. They understood that they were part of something much bigger than just one bee. A euphoric swarmy feeling was developing; they had this boon to share.

Miranda started cooking up the boar's heart and liver as soon as they became available. She set up a fire and makeshift kitchen a little distance from where Alfred was butchering. He decided not to move the boar at all, as it was already positioned well for the initial bleeding. Instead, they set up a temporary camp on the spot where the boar lay dead. Louisa took on any prep-cook job that Miranda, head chef, gave her. Charles went to Rosemary to fetch some herbs for the organ meats, along with other greens. He was the main gopher for this operation, getting things, bringing things, setting things up, and taking direction from Alfred and Miranda.

He wasn't used to taking a supportive role in projects, and it wasn't as easy as he had thought to be the assistant rather than the main mover. If he could read everyone's mind about what they wanted him to do, it would be a lot easier. Or if he could hear better. People were always speaking into his bad ear, and he couldn't just keep saying, "What?"

Miranda and Alfred, cook and butcher, were the main movers of this big event. They collaborated on the menu, Alfred offering to make sausages, smoked meat, bacon, headcheese, and ribs, Miranda working it all into her meal plans.

"Boar's head? It's a traditional Christmas dish," he offered.

"How complicated is that?" Miranda asked.

"Pretty complicated. I have *The Joy of Cooking* at home. There's a recipe for it," Alfred said.

"I don't know. Save the head. We'll figure it out later, after the organ meats and other parts." She returned to her "kitchen" to mix marinades.

It was no small matter to bring glory to the death of this animal, Alfred thought as he sharpened his knives, preparing to cut the fat back for bacon and lard.

"It's like we're being tested. It has been hard, having to make do in times of scarcity, but now that we have the bounty of the boar, that is a challenge, too," Louisa said.

"This is the challenge I trained for since I was a boy. I'm ready for the bounty, and I know you are, too," Alfred said.

"I'm proud of you for rising to the challenge, Alfred. If it weren't for you, providence might have been wasted on us."

"A town without a butcher slips into just ignoring nature. But a hunter does not ignore nature." He looked at Deb. "A hunter is aware of both bounty and scarcity, and knows the joy and pain of each year in the natural world. The butcher is the publisher of the hunter's findings. The butcher transforms beast into meat, presents it and makes the hunter's relationship with nature available to the public as food."

"I can't believe you know or remember that stuff—it's so ancestral," Louisa said.

"That's why I went into politics. I thought I could make changes that would bring back the old ways. I wanted to defend the cultural heritage of my father's father's land."

"What is the baby's name going to be?" Louisa asked him, out of the blue, it seemed.

"I thought you were set on Owen for a boy and Ophelia for a girl?" Alfred said.

"No, I mean last name."

Alfred felt a sting, somewhere indistinguishable in his body. What was she talking about?

"Our last name, of course," Alfred said.

"And what is that?" Louisa tested him.

Oddly, he found he didn't know. He felt like a complete idiot. He thought of his signature recently scrawled at the bottom of an excusal letter for Deb and Tim. What had it said? It was illegible. He could be anybody. No one used last names, but most people remembered what theirs was. Why was she asking this? It seemed to be part of an old fight that he couldn't remember. The last thing he wanted was to be made a fool of when she had just been admiring him in his new heroic role as town butcher. I just have to make something up, he thought.

"Harrington," Alfred said.

"Louisa Harrington," Louisa said, weighing the

words, then, "Ophelia and Owen Harrington . . . Louisa and Alfred Harrington . . . OK, I'll take it. The Harringtons it is!"

She gave Alfred a kiss, which totally baffled and dazed him, then ran over to Miranda to tell all about it. But Miranda put up her hand as soon as she saw Louisa coming.

"Don't tell me," she said. "I'm allergic."

She forgot Miranda had her own man trouble. She felt terrible. *How self-centered I am.* Ramey had abandoned his pregnant wife in the desert in favor of hallucinogenic cacti and a cast of imaginary creatures. How much worse did it get? And yet here was Miranda, strong, faithful, and even happy—as long as no insensitive fool came along and started talking about what men were like.

"What can I do?" Louisa asked, gesturing toward the food.

Miranda smiled. "It's time for the pregnant women to eat the heart. Don't be afraid, it's very good for you."

Charles had been running around like a madman to make this moment possible, shuttling larger parts of the boar to the cave, and smaller parts in marinades like the heart kebabs, sealed in jars, to and from the stream. He fetched cumin, paprika, garlic, and annatto seeds from Rosemary, and oil and vinegar from their own stores.

"One last side to grill here, and then it is best consumed immediately," Miranda said.

"I'm afraid, but it smells good, so it can't be bad," Louisa said.

"Silly girl, this is the best thing since fried chicken . . . I think." Miranda giggled. She hadn't tried the meat yet, but she was drunk on the fumes.

Seven minutes later by the nose, Miranda served up the heart kebabs on a mound of recently gathered greens in a family-sized bowl. They both pulled up to the bowl and ate in contented silence. The men came over and tasted it, but it was understood that the organ meat would go to the pregnant women who needed the fat-soluble vitamins, as Dr. Rosemary advised.

"Better than crickets?" Miranda asked.

"Honestly, I wouldn't know, but this is good. It tastes like real meat," Louisa said.

"About as real as you can get," Miranda replied.

Charles wished he had Ermal's help, running around fetching things for this giant feast. He was used to working with Ermal; they understood each other without too many words. Well, except when Ermal started referring to all that mystical stuff, but Charles had learned to block that out.

Unfortunately, Ermal had passed away last week. He fell off a ladder. Charles had been there when it happened. He carried him inside. Ermal's pulse was gone, but he expected he would fade in and out to have a normal half-life. He left him there, fully expecting to see him again for the next ten years. They had all come to expect that. But when he came back a day later, he saw the same persistent symptoms of actual death he had seen with his parents. The lack of color, the stiffness, the absence of spirit in Ermal's eyes or any other part of his body urged Charles to accept that Ermal had actually died, the first to do so since Charles's parents died in a cyclone before the Great Wobble.

He brought Ermal home and put him in the compost bin with sunflowers that had been growing around his house, and then covered him with hay and more sunflowers on top. It was what Ermal would have told him to do. He was a very down-to-earth man, and this way, his body would become part of their land and help grow new sunflowers. They'd have to leave that compost bin to mature for a few more years, and begin using the other one. There had been no way to have a funeral for Charles's parents when they died; there had been such chaos, and there had been no funerals since.

For old people, birthdays and funerals are alike. People gather and tell stories that illustrate appreciation for the person. They could do this during the feast week, have a remembrance day for him, and invite everyone who knew him well. Not many people knew him well. He was a quiet man. Deb was not close to him. She was not close to many people. "I don't bond," she once said in explanation. That had to be an exaggeration, but there was some truth to it. Ermal was very particular about how things should be done. Charles would miss that. Even Ermal's mystical reasons for why he did things a certain way were so unique you had to miss them.

Grief-stricken, his mind wandered from the tasks at hand, and he thought of Deb. He could lean on her. He felt as if he was the only one who knew what real death was like. Except now Deb knew: she had killed the wild boar. Charles supposed they would all share the taste of death, real final death, the knowledge of total commitment at the feast. The gift of life, both man's and beast's, would be accounted for in their portions, the portions on their plates and in their stories, food for body and soul. He swept away a dust bunny of self-pity before it could hop into a hole. *It's time to fetch Deb.*

Sometimes he thought Deb really did not know what to do with all her good luck. Anyway, he missed her, and she could help him with his errand-boy job. She was much better at these things, the "easy work," he had always called it.

Deb and Francesca were just coming out the front door of the school when Charles came looking for her. She looked like she had just woken up.

"Where have you been, Deb? School was over hours ago," Charles said.

"I fell asleep. Joe had some sort of magical ball, and then when I wanted it, Stevie put a spell on me then I fell asleep . . . and then Francesca delivered some dream mail to me, and it was weird," Deb said.

"Sounds weird. Can you help me out? Alfred and Miranda have me running around doing

256

errands to help with the butchering, cooking, and eventual town-wide feast. I can't hack it alone, I'm burning out," Charles pleaded, imitating Deb's slacker method.

"Never fear." She put up a hand. "I am the rock."

"Rock, my ass," Charles said.

"But what about"—Deb pointed her thumb at Francesca. "She isn't allowed near raw meat."

"We'll drop her off at Joe's. The kids can play Frisbee with her," Charles said.

Deb had started thinking of Tim as a peer and forgot he was a kid. Francesca wagged her whole hind end vigorously at the mention of Frisbee.

"OK." Deb slapped her arm around his shoulders. She loved the "we're pals" feeling the gesture always gave her. Simple as it was, it was somehow the best feeling in the world.

"One of our stops is going to be at the Lecturing Ladies' house to get butcher paper and string," Charles said.

"Magic carpet?" Deb asked.

"That would be helpful. I was concerned the meat would go bad by the time I got back on my bike," Charles said.

Charles couldn't drive a magic carpet. He always seemed a little disapproving of Deb for using one, perhaps a carryover from when they had a truck and he didn't want to waste fuel.

"We can pick one up at Joe's when we drop off

Francesca," Deb said.

"I don't know if they have one—Joe doesn't do much magic anymore."

"I can use any sort of cloth in a pinch."

Charles didn't really want to know more. He didn't like mechanical or mystical things. He liked practical things, like beekeeping, gardening, and building. He had never taken a ride on a flying carpet and was surprised when it turned out to be a lot like riding in a car, except it was completely quiet and you sat as if you were meditating. Posture was important, Deb told him, for proper handling of the carpet on the air currents.

When they arrived back at "camp," the place not too far from where the boar was killed, they came upon Louisa, who was washing and unfolding some partly chewed-up papers.

"We found the papers your boar ate! Alfred is so happy. Most of them are still readable after I wash and straighten them out," Louisa said.

A boulder was checkered with the off-white squares of rescued papers, all in French.

By evening, they had the hog salted away. Louisa cleaned and dried the letters from Alfred's ancestors, rescued from the intestines that Alfred washed out for sausage making. Miranda and Louisa had cooked and eaten the organs. The whole day had been spent bleeding the animal, removing the innards, skinning it, sawing the body into cuts of meat, and hauling it to cool storage in a stream or cave. Some meat had been smoked and left to age in the cave, and ribs had been cut for the next day's barbecue. There was still much preparing and cooking to be done, though, and if the smell of meat smoke wasn't enough to draw people, there were invitations to send out. Louisa agreed to take that on. The main crew would meet for breakfast sausages at the camp again tomorrow and organize a week or so of feasting. Alfred estimated the eating of the fresh meat might go on that long. The preserved meats might be kept longer . . . depending on how hungry people were.

Maybe Deb's honey-man was right about taking care of their social currency. The community spirit evolving around the feast was a far cry from war. *I must have ceased to feel the stealthy progress of hunger until now, in the midst of my deeds of hunger.* The force of hunger drew power from fumes, the mere smell of something, that just-beginning news of something. Hunger crept forward and kept its force ready to win satisfaction against all resistance, internal or external. Hunger motivated and moved each person as if it were food itself. Disguised as nausea, annoyance, protectiveness, resignation, and boredom, hunger animated each life. *Ducks were not even birds until fear gave them the idea to fly; before that, they were floating fish. That pusher, hunger, not just for food but also for communion with people, animals, nature, and spirit, is winning, like the smile of a new friend.*

CHAPTER 21

No invitation other than the smell of sausages cooking was needed. Dezy knew a visit to Deb was due soon anyhow, before the invitation grew stale. Morning suited him. The smell was coming from up the hill, so he proceeded toward the mists. It was pleasant to be outside so early in the morning. The greens and browns in the woods looked deeper before the dew dried, before the sun got too high and white-hot. There were birds singing. What could be more cheerful?

He had lived off the slight nectar of the earliest part of the day since his recovery from Mary's death and Deb's birth. Evening was a time of guilt and shame. Small things were exaggerated: something he'd said or didn't say, uncertainty about his effect. He had done worse things, seen worse things—he felt clean of his past now—it was forgiven, forgotten, purified. It was the day-to-day things, like: Had he snapped at Ruby when she urged him to stop alienating himself and step back inside his family before it was too late? Had he spent his time with her looking off into lonely space rather than looking into her eyes? When these questions came at night, the answers seemed to swell like a psychosomatic infection. In the morning, his soul and body were in fine condition. In the morning, he was at peace.

Deb was drawn too by the smell of the sausages. Wearing her outdoor pajamas, she hiked up the trail in the direction of the encampment and found Miranda cooking bacon and Charles making coffee according to her directions.

Charles did not approve of coffee. "It's a drug," he said. But Miranda was a grown woman, and he didn't want to be a party pooper, not when everything was going so well with everyone joining in for the good of the community. Even Deb and Alfred worked together, sort of. Together, they put the kibosh on war; the papers had been rescued, the pig killed, and the pregnant women had meat.

Deb was happy that she could focus on finishing her book. *Even in the best of times, explanations are needed.* She planted the story seed in the stew of her mind and let it organize itself. A small and fragile frond of literature emerged, and she nurtured it. The book would be the fruit of her experience, the prize for her search for meaning. *In her pajamas, drinking coffee in the woods, sitting by the fire, smelling the sausages sizzling, surrounded by family, she thought: It just doesn't get any better than this.*

She was still getting used to some of her family, like Dezy.

"Hey, my middle-aged kiddo!" he said, fake-punching her in the arm.

"What have you got for me, Dad? The meaning of life?" she teased back.

"Maybe a little of that. I want to tell you later when you're more awake and Miranda's done cooking. Do you know about Jeannette?"

"No, who's Jeannette?"

"Jeannette is Dad's real mom, your other grandmother. She left Jimmy when he was only two years old."

Deb could see Jim fading to her right across the fire. He didn't have much half-life left, and appearances like this would soon cease. He looked so innocent and curious. Deb wasn't sure if Grace had fully crossed over, but it seemed likely she had.

"Nana isn't his real mother? Does he know?" Deb whispered, not sure how Jim/dad would feel about overhearing this conversation.

"I'll tell you more later. It's Miranda's history, too." Dezy had just met his granddaughter an hour ago, and that had gone surprisingly easily. "You both would have liked Jeannette. Mary and I found her in Montréal and visited with her before she died. She was a jazz pianist, a musician like me. Want a biscuit?" he asked, passing her a cast-iron frying pan with corn bread cut into triangles.

It was the best thing Deb had ever tasted. Dezy wandered off, and Jim/dad's faded half-self followed as if to catch up with his son.

Miranda, done cooking the sausages, sat down

next to Deb.

"Next, I'm going to make jambalaya. It's a beans-and-rice dish with sausages. Dezy told me about it," she said, sighing.

"Don't work too hard," Deb said.

"I like making people happy. Everybody is so happy when the food is good and plentiful."

"Are you happy?"

"As long as I don't think about you-know-who, I'm all right."

"Don't worry, he said he'd come back. A man can't live without a woman."

"Who told you that?" Miranda asked.

"Your grandma Grace, actually."

Miranda laughed. "That's what I'm afraid of, that I'll have to pick up the pieces."

"Some pieces are worth picking up—I guess you already decided that."

"Yeah, for better or worse." She took a swig of her coffee and stuck her feet out, finally relaxing.

Maybe it was because Dezy was playing the banjo, singing, "Mammas Don't Let Your Babies Grow Up to Be Cowboys," that nobody noticed the horse. He let out a hello-whinny as he came up the trail, a tan pony with you-know-who on his back. It was Ramey. He looked like he had gone feral: more hair, sweat, and dirt than anything else. He was thinner than usual and his hair was bigger, flowing to his shoulders in electric waves. No one had ever seen him with a beard. His boots, the only souvenir he had traded for out West, looked well used.

It must have been the look on Miranda's face and the way she and the others started toward him, desperate to help. He put up his hand to stop them.

"I'm OK," he said, whispering something under his breath in Arabic only the horse seemed to understand as it gingerly lowered itself to make it easier for Ramey to get off. "I'm just tired and thirsty."

They brought him water and made him a blanket bed under the shade of a nearby tree. Miranda would have liked to talk about what the heck happened out there, but it could wait until Ramey was rested and rehydrated. Clearly, he was close to the edge. She was overjoyed to watch him sip water and sleep at the edge of camp; the same hysterical feeling Deb had when Miranda returned, heartbreaking worry busted over a stupendous jewel of joy.

Dezy motioned Deb and Miranda over. "The time has come. Let me tell you about a woman named Jeannette Lebon, your great-grandmother and great-great-grandmother respectively," Dezy said.

Miranda was eager to listen. No one ever told her anything: that was her main complaint about her parents. Dezy was different, and she welcomed him without asking why he'd been out of the picture for so long and where exactly he'd gone. It was nice to have a grandpa. *Never look a gift horse in the mouth.*

It was one of Grace's sayings. The wonderful thing about early breeding was having several generations alive at the same time. Miranda was lucky to have gotten to know both Great-grandma Grace and Jim/daddy. She was in her thirties, so her child wouldn't have that, but she would be a good mother and make up for it. *We always have to make up for something.*

"Jim/dad grew up as an only child, and his mother's one devotion," Dezy started, and a faded Jim/dad appeared, sitting on a stone, listening. "Only thing was," Dezy continued, "his real mother had been switched for the housekeeper when he was only two years old, and his two older sisters disappeared at the same time. Katie, or Nana as you called her, was not Jim/dad's real mother. Although, what is real? She played the part of mother very well, and she had been in the household since Jim was born. It was only after his real mother, Jeannette, left that Katie became Jim's mother. Dad's dad, Papa Marvin, divorced Jeannette or vice versa. Though it was too shameful to talk about in those days, they rearranged their domestic life in what seemed like a practical way. Jeannette took the two girls to live with her and her new husband up north, and Marvin married the housekeeper, and together they raised Jimmy, as they called him, as if he were their only child."

Dezy put up his finger to show he'd be right back—went to top off his coffee and returned, continuing:

"Katie was the perfect mother. Cook, nurse, and housekeeper, she loved Jimmy, sang to him, plus was beautiful. Jimmy thought it was all pretty great. His real mother, Jeannette, had been quite different. She was an artist, temperamental, aloof, and wild. Jeannette moved often and married four times, producing three more children from her second and third marriages. She was attractive, but with her prominent nose and crooked teeth, not considered a beauty. She traveled, painted abstract landscapes, and played piano. In her old age, she became legendary for her hospitality to other artists, students, and seekers. She had a large circle of friends when she died."

Dezy stopped to let that sink in, drizzling maple syrup over his corn bread and sausages. He took a few minutes to catch up on his eating until a large bumblebee buzzed by, reminding him to keep humming:

"Jim/dad only learned about his real mother and sisters one summer when he was sixteen. It was a little late to mention it, but his parents decided it was time to let him see his other mother and his sisters. They thought he was old enough to survive spending the summer on the outskirts of Montreal with his other family."

"Hold on a second," Miranda said, and brought over a dish of strawberries. "OK."

Dezy picked up again: "The visit did not go

particularly well. His older sisters thought he was a spoiled brat and a big baby; they made fun of him every step of the way. Jeannette also seemed disappointed with the way he had turned out. Jimmy could not bring himself to believe she was his mother, though the family resemblance was undeniable. Her husband at the time, Alexander, tried to bond with him by taking him sailing. Jim got hit in the head with the boom. Something about sailing must have stuck, though, because Jim came back to it in his later years."

Dezy stopped and looked across the fire to see if Jim was still there. Dezy gave a little wave of acknowledgment, and Jim waved back. It was all history now, but Dezy thought everyone in the family should know about Jeannette. She might not have been the best mother, but many of the family talents, passions, and even their various missions in life stemmed from her. Their true inheritance could be traced back to this wild woman.

"I wish we could see her work, or hear her music," Miranda said.

"It's all gone. Your best bet is to listen for her in my music, or look for her in your mother's book, and look for the family resemblance in your baby," he said as he pulled out a photo of Jeannette. She was in her sixties in the picture, and she was standing at an easel, with an inky paintbrush touching the second line of hills in one of her fantastical landscapes.

Deb took the picture and scrutinized it. "She

looks so studious and rebellious at the same time."

"That's her in a nutshell," Dezy said.

"The nut doesn't fall far from the tree," Miranda said, knocking on her mother's noggin.

Jim/dad came over and looked at the photo. "Jeannette understood that the greatest privilege is to be able to walk away from privilege," he said before returning to his place at a distance.

Louisa and Alfred came up the trail together, holding hands.

"Dorme bien?" Miranda asked, trying out her French.

"Oui, oui," Louise answered, happy to have someone to talk to in her first language. She was not as snobby as Alfred, who only liked to converse with native French speakers.

They sat down and were offered coffee, tea, and food as those before them had been offered coffee, tea, and food. After a while, Louisa, Deb, and Miranda left to see the literature preferred by wild boar.

It was a series of letters written in the late 1930s by Alfred's great-great-great-great-grandfather, Maurice, to his children, Bertrand and Jeannette. Though some parts were missing or smeared from their detour through Jeezum's intestines, Louisa knew what they said because Alfred had memorized them all and recounted them to her when she couldn't sleep.

Alfred didn't need the letters anymore to know

what they said. He was only upset to lose them because of their sentimental value. In the handwriting, one could see a shred of Alfred's identity. He recognized his own style of mark making as if handwriting were hereditary.

"This is fascinating," Miranda said. "I don't blame him for being upset."

"Jeannette who?" Deb asked. "Dezy was just telling us about my great-grandmother Jeannette, who I never heard about before."

"Lebon," Louisa said.

"The same name . . ." Miranda said.

"The letters to Jeannette stopped because her father, Maurice, was angry with her for leaving France. He was determined to establish authentic French roots. As a Senegalese, he fought in the wars of France and received French citizenship in return for his service. He studied to be a surgeon, but somewhere along the line, he lost his taste for it and decided to become a butcher. It was a better family business, he said. He met his white wife, Collette, in the market. She was a farm girl who came to the city on weekends to sell produce. It may have been this connection to food and health that convinced him to use his surgeon's skills to cut meat," Louisa mused.

"Tell us more about Jeannette," Deb said.

"She was pink-skinned like her mother, unlike Bertrand, who took more after his father's shining darkness. She fell in love with a Canadian journalist and left France in 1956 to live with him. That didn't last long, though, because he was so fond of her family and French culture in general. For whatever reason, Jeannette seemed only to want to distance herself from her family, the roots they established, and the cultural ground they were planted in," Louise said.

Deb hadn't told anyone about her experiences at the Pylons in the Hills, and she wasn't planning to, but she said, "They told me they tried once already to deliver letters from my ancestors by wild boar, at the Pylons, in the hotel. I think Alfred and I are distantly related, and someone up in the Hills is trying to tell us so."

"It's our Jeannette, isn't it?" Miranda said.

"Ask Dezy and Alfred, they should be able to sort it out. I'm going home to get dressed," Deb said, and left the two to do whatever was next.

"It's a shame for Maurice and Collette that Jeannette left France for good," Miranda said.

"Well, he did establish himself and his family through his son's line. They stayed until Alfred finally left, just in time to experience the Great Wobble in Middleburg. Because of that, he never went back. Instead, he brought France here. Maurice didn't live to find out, though. He lived to be ninety-six. In the 1990s, when he was in his sixties, he stopped writing letters," Louisa said.

"I'm going to go check on Ramey, see what he looks like after his bath—ha, if it is still Ramey under there," Miranda said. "We'll talk more about the letters later with Dezy and Alfred, and see if we can figure out our family tree."

CHAPTER 22

Miranda approached the rock slab near the falls where Ramey had been bathing.

He stretched out now, drying in the sun, wearing jeans and a T-shirt, his hair laid out like a squid still wet, just beginning to puff out at the top as it dried. She wanted to laugh at his comical hairdo but held it in, not knowing if he would be sensitive about his looks after whatever happened in the desert. There was a nice patch of moss on the rock, and she wriggled her toes in it. It reminded her of early fantasies, how pretty she would be in a white dress, walking barefoot on a moss path to say her vows. It didn't quite happen that way.

"How are you doing?" she asked.

"I'm better. Sorry! I know it seems like I went crazy out there, and maybe I did, but that dune just kept moving, and I felt like I knew where I was, like Cairo was just behind it, like I was being called home. But the dune was like a wave, the same wave I was riding. Until the horse found me."

"Tell me about the horse," Miranda said. She

loved horses and would have stayed if she had known there would be horses.

"It's as if we were both trying to conquer the dune but from opposite directions. When I finally got over the dune, I saw him coming in the opposite direction. Something went off in my head, and I realized that in this entire landscape of illusion, this horse was the one thing that was real, so I turned and ran after him. He wouldn't turn around, but he waited for me, and he understood when I spoke in Arabic as if he also had lived in Egypt. I asked him to help me keep my promise, and he brought me here," Ramey explained.

Miranda reclined on the stone slab beside him. The sun, high now, felt like it was baking in the meaning of all that Ramey said.

"I'm glad you found a friend out there, someone from your homeland you can talk to. I was afraid."

"Don't be afraid," Ramey said. "You know I want to be a father. You know I love you." He turned and stroked her cheek. "Farasha amira." In his first language, he called her "butterfly princess."

"Yes." Miranda lay down beside him and smiled. They both fell into a slumber soon after.

"Are you going to eat with us?" she asked when they awoke.

"You know I don't like pork."

"Still? Really? Aren't you hungry?"

"I could hardly bear the smell of it as I was riding up. That's why I looked so terrible. I only persisted because of you. I wanted to be at your side again even though you smell like fried pork!"

"Oh no!" she said, sniffing her hair.

"Just kidding, it's not that bad. You're the one who has a legitimate reason to barf. How do you feel?"

"Surprisingly not bad. Nothing seems to bother me. On the contrary, the pregnancy makes me feel sturdy, confident—not fragile or fussy. Maybe it's the baby's personality coming through. And now that you're back, I feel on top of the world."

Ramey looked like he was going to say something witty, but then just said "aw" and laid his hand on her belly.

Meanwhile, Alfred was organizing the pièce de résistance.

"You have a nice big clearing and an outdoor kitchen at your place, Charles, where people can spread out. Much more suitable for a large outdoor gathering," Alfred said.

"You think we should move the whole shebang down there?" Charles asked.

"Yes, the camp here is too small. Good for immediate processing, but to feed a crowd, you need space for dining, cooking, dancing, storytelling, retreat sitting, and lounging. Besides, we're too close to the Pylons for a big party. The fog is here for a reason," he said, waving his hand in that direction.

Charles sighed. He had just moved all that stuff up there.

"Come on," Alfred said, taking one end of the table Miranda used for food preparation. Charles took the other end, and they began moving things into the glade at the bottom of the gentle mountain.

Once Ramey was on the scene, they were able to enlist the horse. The first load: bags of mangos and cactus.

"There was only one mango tree, but it was very fruitful," Ramey explained. "I lived on cactus the whole time I was there. It's magical. It kept me alive." He braced a piece between his boots and began sawing it laterally with a piece of string from his wrist; when it was sliced open, he showed them the edible part. Inside, the cactus had an opal-like rainbow sparkle. "Pretty, isn't it? And the texture . . . it keeps you going, strengthens you as you chew it." He took a seashell spoon from his pocket and offered them a taste.

Alfred laughed. "How did you ever figure out how to eat this?"

The cactus was ugly from the outside and dangerous to touch.

"It was all there was, until the mango tree. The horse seemed to want it but was afraid for his lips, so I helped him," Ramey said.

"It's like a tonic," Charles said. "I feel like I could move tables all day and never tire."

"It works on all levels. You actually enjoy more whatever you have to do. I had to save some for you all . . . I picked as much as I could on the way out and ate nothing for the last day," Ramey said.

"Thank you on behalf of France," Alfred said.

"You clean up well. I wasn't sure you were our cowboy when you first arrived," Charles said as he patted Ramey on the back.

Just then, the winds picked up, trees swaying. It looked like a hurricane, and the men were scared, holding onto a boulder. It reminded them of the Great Wobble, except that no one felt the urge to leave. They felt somehow a part of this force. Feeling its creativity from within, their fear was mitigated with a bit of trust.

As they watched, cordwood that Deb and Charles kept ready for building flew piece by piece into masonry position to build their house, fixed with solidifying sands. The furnishings and foodstuffs also flew into arrangement. The wind drew an atmosphere of hospitality with slapping wind-hands. It was an orderly and kind storm, a creative and divine storm.

For Charles, who had gone to sea as a boy, this was not completely unfamiliar. You saw strange things at sea. Perhaps it was because his father was long gone that he had a strangely Christian-tinted thought: it's not always easy being close to your heavenly father, though at times, it seems he tries to make it easy for us.

Deb had been at her desk writing when the meaning of the story started to come to her. She was close enough to wrap her arms around it. She sensed her story's nearness, like a ghost, when she heard the sound of a helicopter landing. Of course, it was not a helicopter landing: it was the wind. Dread came into her veins, an awful sense of certainty and uncertainty contained in the same empty thought bubble of inspiration. She was a hunter close to her prey yet unable to see it, knowing that she could lose it or become food herself.

Being in near possession of the story did not provide the complete confidence she had expected. The story's purpose had not changed; it was still a story to be used in the face of a crisis, but the name of the story had changed to The Gift Bearer.

When she opened the front door, what she saw was too confusing to react to, so normal and abnormal at the same time, so good and bad at the same time. It all canceled each other out.

She called to Charles from the doorway, "What are you up to out there?" but it was impossible for him to hear over the roar of the wind. For some reason, they just kept yelling to each other, saying things like, "What?" and "I can't hear you!" and "I can't hear you, either!" They yelled louder and louder.

As the wind subsided, an old woman came out of the hills, someone they had never seen before.

She said, "I live up there." She pointed to the Pylons in the Hills. "And you two"—talking only to Deb and Charles, the screamers—"have been making an awful lot of noise down here. Could you please keep your voices down?"

Deb and Charles apologized; now that the wind was quiet, it was clear how rude they had been, both to each other and to their heavenward neighbors.

"Sorry. We didn't know you were up there," Deb said.

"I have a friend who is a friend of Cicero. Maybe she can help you with your project down here," the old woman said, and waved them off, returning up the hill, presumably to the Pylons.

Deb and Charles looked at each other, relieved, mystified, and grinning over what had just happened. There was nothing to say. The drudgery was finally giving way to the hope and promise they started with when they moved here after the Great Wobble. Alfred and Ramey peered over the top of the split rock as if frozen. The winds had arranged a new, larger fire pit with seating around it and a remodeled kitchen, complete with kindling for the rocket stove and a spit for the fire.

A bright cloud of fog blew gently back and forth over the scene. In one last gentle touch, it cooled and moisturized the vicinity, and everyone present in it. This finally broke the spell for Alfred and Ramey, and things were back to normal. Charles made a fire, and Alfred got ready to cook the roast and grill the ribs.

Louisa, Miranda, and Dezy returned from announcing the feast. Louisa sang out invitations and Miranda backed with bells as Dezy drove the flying carpet through the neighborhood. It was the most fun they'd had in a while.

Deb discovered her story in the shadow of another story called The Sin Eater. The Sin Eater was an old funeral myth, long forgotten and no longer needed. Perhaps all the sins had already been eaten. Deb remembered this story from a TV documentary about life in old-time Appalachia she had seen as a kid. Somehow one story pointed to the other story, like different interpretations of the same thing. Both stories related to feasts and the gathering of people to nourish themselves in a time of need, celebration, ritual, or funeral.

It occurred to Deb that by killing Wild Boar Jeezum, her friend, she was the Gift Bearer, and perhaps in other ways she did not yet understand.

As a hunter, she got a feel for what it meant to be a gift bearer: how even things you didn't like about yourself were gifts, and what it meant to bear them. Something as maddening and personal as her disorderly hair was a gift and burden weighing upon her.

In every sense of the word bearing, I feel my individuality manifest, but perhaps in some senses of the word more than others. Bearing in the sense of delivering and actually giving away still seemed unclear to Deb, even as she found herself witnessing the final commitment of death. In searching for her story, power had come to her, obscure powers of questionable use and worth, yet these gifts demanded attention. *Perhaps life will find a meaning even for the most absurd gifts?*

She knew the time had come to finish it. It was no different than the boar. She was at her desk, ready. All she had to do now was point and shoot. She seemed to sense the words coming from down below, but she didn't understand them. They were in a giant woman lying on the ground like a landscape. She found herself with a man staring at a giant vagina, bulging, stretching, and turning dark purple with the babe's head pushing against the walls. "We have to agree on some words if we are going to deliver this baby. What are we going to call things?" Deb asked the man.

"My wife," he said.

"I sympathize with her, the weirdness of this situation. In bearing a child, your whole personality seems to disappear, and you become a giant vagina, and everyone is looking at it, your most private place. But that's the way it is. What do you call this area?"

"The perineum. It's the boundary of the inner world."

Deb knew his wife from previous dreams. She was a funny woman, like a comedian. Her lips were long, even ribbons of pink. She looked cool with this oddity. She always asked to hear about Deb's "social experiments," and Deb looked forward to talking with her about this, but for now the dream was fading, the giant vagina sinking back into a dark place . . . Deb took another stab at something she thought was missing in her story, and wrote:

> Once upon a time, in a place across the sea, in an alternate reality where you were the narrator of this story that you now find yourself reading, there was a doll all dressed in pink. She was left behind when a family moved out of the bungalow that your family had just moved into. The new house made your parents invisible. You saw your mother's phone doodles on the kitchen table. You saw your father's coffee cup and discarded socks by the sofa. But you saw your parents even less now than before they moved away from Lake Paradime.

> There were three sisters, and you were the middle child. In most fairy tales, the oldest or the youngest solves the problem, but since you were narrating the story, you changed it so that you could be the heroine.

Your name was Elaine. Your older sister, Jody, couldn't care less, but you saw her every day, and loved her anyway. Your younger sister, Buffy, was really cool and could be talked into anything. She was your action figure.

One day, you asked Buffy, "Have you noticed that our parents are invisible?"

She laughed. "That can't be. We must not have noticed them coming and going. See, look, there are groceries. Mom must have been here. We just didn't see."

Perhaps Buffy didn't grasp the idea of "invisible."

"Let's eat the evidence," you said, taking a bag of grapefruit from the cupboard. We ate the whole delicious bag of expensive grapefruit. Their skins, forbidden with their empowering, now empty sections, were scattered everywhere. Yet did you ever get in trouble? No.

Buffy and Elaine became certain they lived only with ghosts and with Jody, who couldn't care less.

"Did Mom or Dad give you the doll?" you asked Buffy.

Buffy said, "No."

"Let's abandon her," you said.

"She's already abandoned, and she doesn't look real anyway. She's stuffed with beans and her clothes don't come off," Buffy protested.

Buffy wanted a baby that could really eat, drink, and go pee. The doll seemed like a mad joke to her. She called it "pink bluff."

"No, let's abandon her officially. Wrap her up in a white cloth with only her head peeping out, and leave her with a note someplace where she will find real parents," you said.

Buffy and Elaine took the long way back from school, planning to find a place where people might decide to take an abandoned baby home. They asked Jody if she wanted to come, but she just blew her hair out of her face and said, "I couldn't care less!"

They walked to the docks near a café their parents used to take them to before they became invisible. Elaine played in the water and almost got taken out to sea before she realized that she better paddle to shore while she still could. Buffy wanted to play in the water, too, but was too scared to go through the dark tunnel leading there, so she waited at the gate in front of the tunnel for Elaine to return. You were not Elaine anymore.

They went to the café and left the baby. As they headed out, it started to snow.

Buffy had found a magic kitten

along the way.

"How do you know it's magic?" Elaine asked.

"See how he's following me," Buffy said, "and how his little black tail points straight up?"

That didn't prove anything to Elaine, but the cat was black, and black cats were magic for witches. Who knows, maybe Buffy was a witch. But it turned out the cat was magic because it made their parents suddenly appear. They were adamant that the cat go back to whoever he really belonged to. Elaine found their sudden passion suspicious. Buffy was sure that since the cat followed her of its own free will, it belonged to her.

Since Buffy sort of belonged to Elaine, Elaine surmised that her place was to defend Buffy's position and to co-parent the kitten. Elaine asked Jody to weigh in on their side, but Jody only said, "I couldn't care less!" and slammed the door of her room. When the parents implored Jody to help Buffy return the cat, she declined, saying that it really didn't make any difference to her if they had a cat now.

Yes, they had a cat now. They had parents who didn't want a cat, but who were now present and vocal.

Deb was saddened by this little vignette that sprang from deep dream space, like the confessions of Mummy Woman whose bandages turned to living skin as Deb held and rocked her. Mummy Woman's hurts told of the troubled child, lost and lost again.

The attention Deb's dubious gifts demanded was "bearing." Gifts and injuries were often linked. Jacob, who wrestled with the angel, was blessed, but afterward, was also lame.

The final giving came after unpacking and accepting all the gifts of life's journey; it came with eternal being calling your name and asking for your embrace.

Alfred would translate the letters from her ancestors, delivered by wild boar. They had seemed so different, so foreign to each other; their skin did not even match, yet their common blood could be traced back through Jeannette. Deb counted her blessings, trying not to dwell too much on judging their worth: the wild boar, the cougars, sweet cicely, Tim's friendship, the grass in the field, telepathic thought, Louisa's strange story, rainbow vision, the blue light, Mummy Woman. It went on and on. Who knew how these things might at some future time influence the group? For now, she would not abandon any gift, no matter how absurd.

Gift Bearers bear their gifts on behalf of the

group. One who bears gifts may be thought of as suffering, enduring, abiding, tolerating, containing, holding, assuming, accepting; as the earth accepts our bodies when we die, as the tree bears the weight of its fruit, as the mother bears the child, as a porter bears supplies. The Gift Bearer may be completely passive, delivering only if and when it is needed. Even old age holds potential. The gift is to be borne: that is the essence.

What is needed is not to avoid crisis but to let the crisis bring out the gifts that you are meant to bear, and ultimately to give.

⤷ CHAPTER 23 ⤶

The week of feasting and celebration changed things for Deb and Charles. Their work had seemed endless and the fruits of their labor too late, but now new hope and purpose cropped up in their lives. The house, its roof covered with drought-resistant sedums and mounds of flowering thyme for the bees, fit perfectly into the land like a living being. Miranda and Ramey would have a safe place to grow their family, and Deb and Charles would continue living in the hangar, home enough for them after all these years. The motorcycle ran out of fuel, which could not be replenished, so Deb and Charles created a memory garden around it. They planted yellow roses and created a pool from a natural spring that trickled down the rocks from the hills.

Despite this, Deb was not satisfied. Her mission did not feel complete. Hideous wounds of abandonment came from all sides as she searched for her story: the time Alfred would have left had Louisa not hit him on the head, Jim/dad's desertion, his mother at the bottom of it, Dezy blinded when his young wife died, Miranda's unbearable tears when Ramey left her in the desert. Deb had not been spared abandonment either: the pain of being excluded and ignored, the uncertainty of acceptance, the struggle to find a place humane enough to meet her needs. *Where is the shopkeeper in this gift shop of life?*

How do you solve abandonment? Don't commit suicide! Any strategy is good as long as you don't give up. The wounds of abandonment are not pretty. They make you feel guilty and repulsed, but if you take a good look at them, you can heal yourself. Deb would not abandon herself or her gifts. She would have compassion for all of the wounded, even herself, even those she had wounded. She would forgive the acts of the wound. That was how you stood up for yourself. She knew it. She knew all this, yet hadn't taken the time to know Mummy Woman as herself. She always kept moving, glossing over any problems, especially if they were her fault.

I'll be washing, hanging up to dry, and folding these experiences from my past, she thought, perhaps even ascertaining treasures from those darker times. I have a place now where I can do that. My home is now complete with family, nature, and neighbors both spiritual and earthly.

In a dream, she traced the river of her life to a fork on a map, but then saw that what looked like a fork was actually the river turning into the ocean. The river disappeared into the ocean with a whispering swish, its name swallowed. . . *I thought I was at a fork in my river . . . but I am in the Delta, a watery labyrinth where many things can be sent to sea.*

The ocean, she had assumed, would reject her and her gifts. A sting of rare tears scorched pink trails down her cheeks. She felt as if it were impossible to solve her puzzle alone.

When she tried to think of someone who might possibly help—even if actual publication was an entirely lost art—the face of an old mentor came to mind. Various things had separated them, but she knew he existed. Using an old address she still had for him, the professional one, she simply asked for help. His answer was curt: "No, too busy right now." Of course, she understood, in the worst way, that no one in a position to help had time for her.

She turned her communication stone to Tim and sent a mangled phrase of desperation. That night, she received a steady stream of Tim's sympathy. A picture came of his hands placed on her, and from his hands a gentle healing energy. His veins were white, the skin near his veins flashing blue and then red. She knew him by his colors, like a superhero, like some innocent memory of the USA. It was nice to have a friend. She couldn't have asked Charles because he was not in the same field. What happened in the field could only be shared with those in the field—though not everyone in the field was a friend. Some were neutral, some were enemies, but all were bonded by the field, their profession, or their calling.

And why have I tasted this, why have we all tasted this worst pus of hell, abandonment? There is no honesty in denial; there is no wholeness with missing links. The knowledge of who we are and where we come from must be restored, reknit in our bones, so that we can resume our places and be ourselves, without fear of mockery or dismemberment.

The cool mornings of fall brought touches of warm color to the trees at the edge of the forest where they had their summer fun. The weather, made in the pattern of something long lost, before a hotter sun slackened New England into a wilted version of itself, was like a well-known song. She couldn't be sure the four seasons were back, but the days came one by one, warm while the sun was high, and cool on either end. She hadn't known how much these seasonal expectations were a part of her, even though they had been absent for a very long time. It was as if all this time, she had been in a slightly bad mood just because the weather had been a bit off, and now it was lifting.

The last weeks were always the hardest. Louisa, bored to tears alone in her singing room, coughed.

No music, no people, no opera. She lined up everything on her dressing table as if the objects were an audience, a silk scarf hung over the mirror like a curtain. She coughed again, experimenting with the sound. Expelling puffs of air, shooting breath up against her throat, she barked like a dog. The sound, to imagine it visually, was like texture with no color; a percussive wind without vowels or words. Her assembled objects listened dutifully, she imagined, moving together and swaying in her tabletop puppet play. Lecturing in conspiring cough sounds, she found herself dizzy from lack of in-breaths and knocked her audience down.

At one time, she had known the lyrics to a song called "The Wild Boar." Like a terribly itchy memory she couldn't quite locate, somewhere in the air, the song was floating. If she could catch it and pull it down to earth, she could rescue it from the depths of collective memory. The boar, unclean and yet holy, is a creature highly charged with spiritual power. She paced a beat on the floor, soaking up its devouring power, its producing power, and its feminine moon power. "But reconciled among the stars!" The line bobbed up from the rhythm of her walking and thinking.

She played with it, sniffing and listening to the sound, letting it vibrate in the back of her nose. She snorted with hungry laughter, like a pig. She wanted its song, something mythological, some sort of drama involving the underworld. She wanted something to sing about, something to give her voice to.

It began to get dark and she was getting restless. The breathing had moved something inside her. She walked outside and saw a few red leaves that had fallen. They seemed so strange, like goldfish swimming in airy clover, long dashes in pillowy greens. She kneeled to admire them, collecting some of the leaves. The shapes contrasted in such a lively way. Slivers of scarlet scalloped through clouds of green. She remembered a fragment from T.S. Eliot's *Four Quartets*:

> We move above the moving tree
> In light upon the figured leaf
> And hear upon the sodden floor
> Below, the boarhound and the boar
> Pursue their pattern as before
> But reconciled among the stars.

Squatting with her rare ruby handful of fall leaves, the first to fall in many years, she felt a great wetness and thought she had peed. Feeling a bit on the wobbly side, it occurred to her this could be the sign, the symbol, and the thing itself. My water has burst, she thought.

She inched forward, one wide step at a time. The moving was happening in painful waves, beginning the nearly impossible change. Francesca saw Louisa's strange walk, and with her white tail waving like a flag of surrender, went to get Alfred from his study. Louisa made her way to the rocker and sat, wondering how much longer it would be. She screamed. She had never made such an ugly sound in all her life, but somehow it was satisfying. I suppose I can say whatever I like, she thought; in this sort of pain there are no rules. And she frightened everyone out of the house—except Deb.

When Deb heard the scream, she had been walking reluctantly to their house with questions for Alfred about the publishing. She hated to bother him, what with his pregnant wife and all. She just wanted to have a reason to stop by, it seemed.

Alfred was in the garden, stammering about getting Rosemary, when Deb remembered her dream of the giant vagina.

"Alfred, calm down, we can help with the delivery ourselves. Rosemary's too far away," Deb said.

"Her water has broken!" Alfred said.

"That's what I mean. Hear her terrible screams? We have to be with her—the baby could come VERY soon!" Deb said.

So they went back and did what they could do: boiled water, put down clean sheets.

"Shhh, don't wear yourself out, Louisa, save it for your opera. Just rest, go to sleep between contractions, dream little dreams," Deb told her. It was the same thing her midwife had told her years ago during her long labor with Miranda.

"You're unbelievably beautiful. The baby's coming, I can see its head!" Alfred said.

"Are you sure that's the head actually coming through, or is she just bulging?" Deb whispered to him as she went down to look.

"It's something . . . maybe an elbow . . . I better push it back," he said.

Deb nodded. Alfred reached in and quickly, expertly pushed back the baby's arm so that the head would have more room to come out. Shortly after, they saw a tiny portion of the head peep through. Alfred started remembering the kinds of things they might need and rattled them off to Deb: receiving blanket, bulb syringe, baby hat . . .

"Breathe like a horse, let your lips go loose, relax, long out-breaths . . . pant," Alfred coached.

Louisa liked the horse-breath best. That was the advice for her because there was no time for sleeping. Hers was turning out to be a quick labor, the dark wet hair already visible.

"I think I can help," Deb said. It was just a feeling she had, that she should place her hands there around the perineum like in her dream; sending Reiki so the baby could come out without hurting Louisa. She knew there were hormones in the body that helped with this, but didn't want to regret not listening to her intuition.

Deb focused healing energy on the perineum, the boundary of the inner world, the door between chapters of life, between aquatic and terrestrial life.

She was precious, like a little black-eyed pea, so small and quiet, still curled in the fetal position like a bean, her dark hair in curled wet lines. She was a little treasure. Without hurrying to cut the cord, Alfred put Ophelia on her mother's breast. Little Ophelia gripped her mother's pinky, and they looked into each other's eyes.

The baby started to suckle, and all was well.

I'm not just a finder of things, not just a hunter, writer, detective, or story wrangler. I'm a guide. I helped a baby out of the womb and into life, I killed the boar and brought him to his death, and I've been a mother and a professor. Now I am at the end of my river, in the delta of eternity's ocean. To guide others across these dimensions is the next logical step. The crisis of my vocation brought the gifts I was meant to give.

Even if Deb wasn't sure when or if she would be called upon, she knew the Way now. She could dig a trench between lands and connect them with circulating water, recreate the sky from over there so that it was over here. She would be waiting at the edge to say, "After you" to the next seeker.

There is no honesty in denial; no wholeness with missing links. The knowledge of who we are and where we come from must be reknit in our bones, so we can resume our place and be ourselves, without fear of mockery or dismemberment.

The next evening, around the fire, Dezy asked:

"Does anyone have any last things to share? As the body of the wild boar finds redistribution in us, as we take our gathered strength back to our individual lives, I want to invite anyone who has not shared everything that they have to share to come forward and . . . well, be saved." Dezy knew not everyone was a born-again Christian and was trying to span a certain need that he understood from his involvement with closing drawn-out group rituals.

"I do," Deb said, retrieving her stack of papers, clipped together in three parts. Jim/dad, sitting in his usual spot to the right, across the fire, spoke: "Your attention to this dark part of my life makes me feel like someone knows and cares. I have read the first part of your book, and I want to read the rest on the other side." He held out his hands as if he could barely move and needed her to do the rest.

A watery orb of blue light came down from the hills. It was Ermal, etched in light, made of fog. He said to Deb, "Imitate your father's recovery, not his fall." He threw an ax that flew far away in the most illogical and beautiful fashion. It came back to him, harmlessly returning to his hand.

Watching Ermal gather his wood this way amazed Deb, and she asked with admiration, "How do you do that?"

"Just throw your ax off to the west," he said.

Deb smiled and walked over to her father, giving him the book. He hugged her one last time.

Jim/dad turned toward Ermal, whose blue light opened into a path. Grace was there, too, waving. As Jim/dad disappeared into the bright blue folds of the fog, he and Ermal and Grace rolled into a cloud and drifted up the mountain.

Not long after, Alfred came up to Deb and said, "I assume that wasn't your only copy?"

"My only paper copy. I have it on memory card."

"You better go into town and print up another copy. My relatives in France will want to know all about their American and Canadian sons and daughters."

"That's not what it's about," Deb said.

"I know what it's about. You think I don't talk to anybody?"

Deb smiled. It was one of the things that had made her suspicious about him, the way he talked to everybody, sometimes through someone else.

"I'm going to publish it, just like in the old days, when news and novels were published," Alfred said.

"How do you know it's any good? You haven't read it," Deb said.

"You are the lonely hunter, I have seen you do not miss your mark," Alfred said.

"Well, Uncle Alfred, I guess it's the least you

can do for your old double great-aunt." She stuck out her hand to seal the deal.

"Small world," he said, his eyes watering.

Louisa, surprised, asked, "You crying?"

"My eyes are watering, I'm getting old. That's just what happens to old men," he said, trying to be patient with her innocence.

"No more flex time?" she asked.

"Did you not get the blue light memo? It is no longer cool to stick around after the party is over," he said.

"It's not over till it's over . . ." she said, and started singing: ". . . Those were the days, my friend . . ."

Dezy was right behind her on the harmonica. Charles went to Deb and offered his hand. The song seemed like a good one to dance to.

Acknowledgements

A deep thanks to readers of this novel's early and later drafts: My friend and neighbor Ambika Gibbs, parents Sally and Bob Eckles, and friend Jonathan Lethem. Their feedback and encouragement have been almost essential. I am glad I didn't have to do without it. Thanks also to Marcia Trahan for her excellent editing services. Many thanks to my sisters Margaret and Ruth Eckles. Ruth helped me get rid of extra words, and Margaret was the cover and formatting guru. Everlasting thanks to my life's companion Ross Conrad for always being there willing to help with most anything from reading, giving feedback, copy editing, financing, leaving me alone when I'm writing, and most of all for putting up with me for the past eight years. Thanks also to all my supporters from the book's Indiegogo campaign: Kate Maher, Kathleen Smith, Jennifer Vyhnak, Lisa Gagnon, Kent Hikida, Heather Seeley, Regina Walker, SJ Chiro, Victoria Gilbert, Jessamyn West, Nancy Gilbert, Janet Van Fleet, James Wesner, Marilyn Gold, Mary Martin, and many Anonymous people. Thanks to my daughters Ana and Thea for their support and inspiration. Thanks to Dancing Bee Press for stepping up, Alice Eckles for sticking by me, and to the giver of life without which none of this would be possible.

ALICE ECKLES

Alice Eckles is the author of a Phrase Book for Spiritual Emergencies, and publishes artisanal batches of poetry and prose that she sells from her honey booth at farmers markets and other events since she is also a beekeeper, shiitake grower and homesteader. Her writing has appeared in a number of publications including The Seattle Review and Nomads Choir. After studying sculpture and printmaking at Bennington College, she went on to earn her Master's of Education from Antioch new England Graduate School, with Waldorf Certification. She worked as a professional artist and art teacher in Vermont for many years before devoting herself to writing. Eckles has participated in a Vermont Studio Center Residency and the Bread Loaf Writer's Conference. She lives with her life's companion Ross Conrad in a yurt without electricity or running water, where they plan to build a cordwood house.